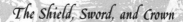

The Shield, Sword, and Crown

SHIELD OF STARS

Hilari Bell

Simon & Schuster Books For Young Readers
New York London Toronto Sydney

SIMON & SCHUSTER BOOKS FOR YOUNG READERS
An imprint of Simon & Schuster Children's Publishing Division
1230 Avenue of the Americas, New York, New York 10020
SIMON & SCHUSTER BOOKS FOR YOUNG READERS is a trademark of Simon & Schuster, Inc.
Book designed by Lucy Ruth Cummins
The text of this book was set in Celestia Antigua.
Interior illustrations by Drew Willis
Manufactured in the United States of America
2 4 6 8 10 9 7 5 3 1
Library of Congress Cataloging-in-Publication Data
Bell, Hilari.
Shield of stars / by Hilari Bell.
p. cm. — (The shield, sword, and crown ; bk. 1)
Summary: When the Justice he works for is condemned for treason, fourteen-year-old and semi-reformed pickpocket Weasel sets out to find a notorious bandit who may be able to help save his master's life.
ISBN-13: 978-1-4169-0594-3 (hardcover)
ISBN-10: 1-4169-0594-4 (hardcover)
[1. Conduct of life—Fiction. 2. Robbers and outlaws—Fiction. 3. Kings, queens, rulers, etc.—Fiction. 4. Fantasy.] I. Title. II. Series: Bell, Hilari. Shield, the sword and the crown; bk. 1.
PZ7.B38894Shi 2007
[Fic]—dc22
2005035571

FIRST EDITION

To Joyce and William Griffen, aka
Aunt Kelly and Uncle Bill, who have cared
about my writing since the beginning.

CHAPTER 1

THE TWO OF STARS

The Two of Stars: imminent reprisals.
May also indicate payment of a debt, or an arrest.

"If this is treason," said Weasel, "should you be writing it down?" He tucked the quill back in the inkwell and rubbed his cramping hand.

The shutters had been closed to conceal the light in the justice's study, so no one walking the puddle-strewn cobbles would wonder why such an important man was awake so late—several hours had passed since the city clock chimed midnight.

But despite the danger, sealing in the light of hearth and candle made the book-filled room feel warm and safe. As if the night were shut out, instead of light imprisoned.

"Ah, but you'll note that I'm not writing it," said Justice Holis serenely. He laid down his book so readily that Weasel knew he'd only been pretending to read it. "Putting treason on paper in your own hand would be both dangerous and foolish. That's why you're doing it for me."

Weasel snorted. "Seriously, sir, aren't you taking a huge chance if one of these letters is intercepted? Why not send a messenger?"

His employer leaned back in his comfortable chair and regarded Weasel thoughtfully. Light glinted on his spectacles.

"That's a fair question. The answer is that a letter, sent by post in a plain wrapper, is less likely to arouse suspicion than half a dozen men galloping through the countryside. Not to mention the difficulty of finding that many men who wouldn't sell me out to Regent Pettibone for the reward."

"Reward?" asked Weasel. "What reward?"

"The reward the regent would most certainly give anyone who brought to his notice a conspiracy to break his power, and remove—"

"How big a reward?"

Holis gave in and laughed. "Don't bother. I know you won't betray me."

"Are you sure about that?"

Holis smiled. "It's a good distraction, but not good enough. Back to work. The sooner those letters are posted, the sooner we're both safe. Safer, I should say."

The justice knew him too cursed well. Weasel picked up the quill and wiped off the excess ink on the lip of the bottle before he wrote.

I have spent some time with the young man in question. He is a reserved boy, but I think I have made a start in gaining his trust. . . .

This was the fifth copy he'd written, so Weasel knew the rest of the letter's contents. The confirmation that Regent Pettibone had complete personal control over both the palace and the city guards and was slowly gaining influence in the army, and even the navy. That he was also growing more popular with the common folk here in the city, despite the fact that the country rustics generally didn't care for him. Though Justice Holis didn't call them rustics.

Weasel lifted the quill again to yawn. "What does it matter what the bumpkins think? Or even the townsmen? As long as Pettibone controls the guard and the army he can do as he likes. He doesn't have to care what anyone thinks."

"Really?" Holis asked dryly. "Will you feel the same if my friends and I succeed in replacing him with a new regent? We're doing it because we *think* he's a bad influence on the young prince, and a bad ruler for Deorthas."

"Yes, but you've all got money, and power, and the law on your side too," Weasel objected. "As long as that 'Concordance of Nobles' thing is still on the books."

"Oh, it's on the books," said Holis. "If all the nobles in Deorthas meet with leaders of the church, and two-thirds of them agree that the king's close adviser is harmful to Deorthas and its king, then his position will be filled by another. Mind, the last time this law was envoked was almost a thousand years ago . . . but it's still on the books."

"And it says 'king,' not 'prince,'" said Weasel, who had taken the trouble to locate the passage in one of Holis' books. A dusty book, titled A History of the Ancient Laws of Deorthas. "And it talks about advisers, not a regent."

"I'm sure Regent Pettibone will point out both those things," said Justice Holis mildly. "Which is why we need to be ready for him with a firm majority in the nobles, and the support of the country folk, too."

"The bumpkins' support isn't going to be worth much, when the guard comes for you," Weasel muttered.

This could get Justice Holis hanged. And his clerk along with him!

Fortunately, Weasel had a backup plan prepared. In a few more months, he'd probably have improved his talents as a forger enough to make a living at it. He could have used a different hand on these letters, which might be safer—but it would mean admitting that he'd been studying the forger's trade, and that was a confession Weasel didn't want to make.

Pickpockets had to keep in practice, and Weasel hadn't been able to use his old craft for more than three years. Not since the day Holis had captured Weasel's hand wiggling into his pocket. So a new career was clearly in order, and a good forger made more than a pickpocket. Forgery was safer, too. Mind, it was almost as dull as being a law clerk, but you couldn't have everything. He didn't *want* to be a law clerk, though he knew Justice Holis would be disappointed. . . .

Sometime in the last three years, not disappointing the justice had become important to Weasel.

"The country folk have a different kind of power," Holis said, interrupting Weasel's thoughts. "Look at all the trouble the Falcon has caused, and he's only one bandit. The townsmen have power too. In fact, at the heart of it, people are the only thing that matters."

"More than law?" asked Weasel curiously.

"Who do you think makes the law? And why are legal cases tried individually, by people? But fortunately for us, the country folk have always given their allegiance to the true king. That's what makes the young prince so important."

"The 'young prince' is fifteen," said Weasel. "He's a year older than I am."

"In years, yes," said the justice. "But I'm afraid that in some ways he's younger than you ever were. Which is one of the problems with Pettibone. I fear the prince has been . . ."

"Spoiled rotten?"

" . . . badly raised," Holis corrected firmly. "And as I was saying, the country folk will be loyal to him. Although . . . I wish the sword and shield hadn't been lost. They were only symbols, but symbols have a kind of power too. I'm told that there's unrest now, even in the countryside. If the sword and shield were found, that might settle. Which, of course, is why the regent has posted a reward for them."

"A reward? How big—All right, all right, I'm working."

"You might as well," Holis told him. "The sword and shield were lost centuries ago. To a burglar, I understand."

Weasel grinned. "I thought one of the old kings lost them at cards."

Holis laughed. "I've heard that one too, but it seems . . . unlikely. The sword and the shield were the symbols of the true king from the beginning of Deorthas' history. It would be incredibly irresponsible to gamble with them."

"You think kings can't be irresponsible?"

"Most of them aren't."

"Prince Edoran would be."

Holis started to deny it, then sighed. "He might, if he continues the way he is now. Which is why you're writing these letters. Or more accurately, not writing them."

Weasel dipped the quill again. "With an irresponsible king, the smart thing to do is stay out of his way."

"The trouble with you, lad," said Holis mildly, "besides the fact that you're not working, is that you have no social conscience."

"I can write and talk at the same time," said Weasel, proving his point as his pen moved across the page. "And judging by what I'm writing, a social conscience could get a man hanged. I care about me first, me second, and nobody else. It's safer that way."

"Is it?" Holis asked, falling, as he always did, for a philosophical argument. "Or does your isolation render you more vulnerable, because you don't—"

Bam. Bam. Bam. Someone pounded on the door. Weasel flinched so violently that he jostled the desk, spilling ink over the fifth letter in a dark flood.

"Open in the name of the law!" a rough voice shouted.

"Quick, the letters!" Holis plucked the stained one from under Weasel's hand as he spoke. "I'll burn them, you answer the door." He crumpled the papers into a loose bundle. "Delay as long as you can. In fact . . . "

He reached out with one hand and pulled Weasel's shirttails out of his britches.

"Take off your shoes and stockings. Make it look like they woke you up. Rumple your hair and—"

"I've got it," said Weasel. He could feel his heart racing. "I'll give you as much time as I—"

Bam. Bam. Bam. "Open in the law's name, or we'll break down this door!"

"I'm coming," Weasel shouted. He kicked off his shoes as he ran, and snatched them up to toss behind the chest that sat in the short hallway beside the stairs. His long stockings slowed him more; he hopped and stumbled as he tugged them off and thrust them into his pocket.

Bam. Bam. Bam.

"I'm coming!" he cried again, running his fingers through his hair. With his shirt out and his feet bare, it should look like he'd just tumbled out of bed and thrown on some clothes. His eyes wouldn't be sleep-swollen, but there was nothing he could do about that, and—

Crash! The ram shook Justice Holis' heavy door, and the lamp glass clattered. Weasel hurried forward.

"I'm opening up!" he shouted, pulling the bolts as slowly as he dared. "The God rot you—"

The door swung open.

"—it's the middle of the night!" Weasel put all the indignation he could into his voice, but his heart sank.

Ten men stood on the threshold, wearing the green and white uniforms and black tricorne hats that marked the city guard. At least they carried the cudgels they wielded when they patrolled, instead of pistols, but a full troop such as this wasn't needed for an inquiry. A full troop meant a search, and probably . . .

"What do you want here?" Weasel demanded, hoping he

sounded stuffy instead of terrified. "This is the home of Justice Holis, a most influential—"

"We've come to see the justice," said a man, pushing his way through the guards. He was clad in a good brown coat and plain waistcoat, rather like the clothes Weasel wore when the justice wanted him to look respectable—though this man's coat was better cut, and made of finer cloth. "Take us to him. Now."

He stepped into the hall, thrusting Weasel back, and the guardsmen came in after him.

"I don't know where he is." Weasel's glare wasn't entirely feigned. He'd opened the cursed door. There was no reason for them to be rude. "He was still reading when I went to bed, but he's probably asleep by now."

"In fact, I'm not," said Justice Holis calmly. He left the study and moved down the narrow hall, leaving the door open behind him—just like a man with nothing to hide, Weasel noted approvingly. Even in the beginning, he had never mistaken Justice Holis for a stupid man. Unrealistic, impractical, and way too trusting, but not stupid.

"How can I assist you, Master Darian? Or perhaps I should say, how may I assist the regent?"

Weasel didn't know the man, but he recognized the name from Holis' correspondence. Regent Pettibone's clerk. The cold air pouring through the open door, damp from the rain that had ended only a few hours ago, was sufficient excuse for Weasel's sudden shudder.

He cast the guards a disgusted look and went to close the

door, just as the clerk of a good, innocent man would. He was reaching for the knob when Master Darian grabbed his wrist and twisted it, turning his right hand toward the light.

The small black stains on his fingers looked like blood.

"Ink," said Darian. "You've been writing something."

"I'm a clerk," said Weasel, trying to tug his hand free. "I write things all the time."

"I tell you to wash your hands all the time too," said Holis. "For all the good it does."

Darian's eyes went to the study door and his grip tightened. He stalked down the hall, dragging Weasel behind him. Holis fell back before them, into the room, and the guards followed.

The study was too well-lit for a man reading alone, Weasel thought, as his gaze tracked after Master Darian's. But he saw nothing that would reveal the truth.

Darian's gaze fell on the tall desk. The stool was pushed back, as Weasel had left it, but the quill lay neatly in its slot and the inkwell stood upright and capped.

"Writing," Master Darian breathed.

"Can I have my hand back?" Weasel asked. Master Darian ignored his words, pulling Weasel over to the desk. It looked tidy, except . . .

Weasel stifled a gasp. Darian reached out and ran the fingers of his free hand over the dark stain. They came away black with ink.

"I told you to clean that up this afternoon," said Holis severely. The guards might have believed it, but a clerk would know how quickly spilled ink dried.

"You were writing something. Here, in this room." Master Darian's eyes searched once more. Weasel took a steadying breath and willed his wrist to go limp in the clerk's strong grasp, moving with the man so he felt no resistance. It was an old trick, but reliable, and it worked this time, too—the hard grip loosened.

"But if you were working on something, where did you hide it? You can't have gone far. Guards, spread out and search . . . "

His gaze found the hearth.

"Rot!" He let go of Weasel and ran forward, grabbing for the bundle of paper. It was visible behind the logs only because it blazed so high.

Darian snatched his hand back, swearing, and reached for the poker and tongs.

Two of the guards had seized Holis when Master Darian cried out, but the justice was too wise to struggle. He never even glanced at Weasel, his gaze fixed on the small drama at the hearth.

The rest of the guards were also watching Master Darian as he dragged out the flaming papers. They tumbled onto the rug, scattering glowing embers. There wasn't much left of them.

"Put them out! Put them out! Hold him!"

He couldn't help the justice if he got arrested too.

Weasel eased backward. The cold draft on the back of his neck guided him to the open door as surely as his eyes might have. Only when he'd passed through the doorway did he turn and spring silently down the hall, not even pausing to retrieve his shoes.

The front door was still open, and rain-scented air enveloped Weasel as he stepped into the night. He had a few minutes, at most, before they noticed his absence. But even as he raced toward the street, the walkway's freezing cobbles bruising his feet, some part of him wanted to be there, beside his master, sharing his fate.

Which was probably the most lunatic notion he'd ever come up with—and that was saying a lot! Weasel cursed his own foolish heart as he turned off the road and stepped onto a low brick wall that lined a neighbor's flowerbed.

In spring or summer it wouldn't have mattered, but the last of the autumn flowers had finally died, and some busy gardener had just spaded and raked the beds. The marks of Weasel's bare feet would be plain as print. Fortunately, the brick wall ran right up to the side of the house, where ornamental statues and bushes framed the front door.

Delivering papers to that door, as a respectable clerk, Weasel had barely noticed them. But not so very long ago, he had made a living in a trade where pursuit by angry victims, and sometimes by patrolling guards, had been a part of his daily life. Weasel still noted hiding places, and escape routes, wherever he went.

A long step took him onto the base of a statue. Weasel clung to it as if the marble dame were his scarce-remembered mother, as he worked his way around and then dropped into the narrow space between the pedestal and the wall. When he recaptured his breath and poked his head out, a screen of brush shielded him from the street.

In the daylight he might have been visible through the bare branches. But now clouds drifted across the moon, and the light from the streetlamps, which burned all night in this wealthy neighborhood, didn't reach into the shadows by the wall.

The wet stone against his back and feet made him shiver, but he didn't have to wait long.

They marched down the street in two columns, the guards' boot heels making an amazing racket in the quiet night. Justice Holis walked between them. His expression was placid, but Weasel knew the justice well enough to read fear in the stiffness of his posture. Master Darian followed, like a sinister shadow in his dark coat. And, the God be praised, not one of them even looked in Weasel's direction.

At least they'd allowed Holis to put on a coat. He was an old man, and damp was bad for his lungs. If they put him in a cell . . .

Weasel gritted his teeth and forced himself to think. He didn't know if they'd succeeded in salvaging any of the letters, but the fact that they'd come in such force, prepared for an arrest, meant they already had the evidence they needed.

Weasel had to . . . to what?

Now might be a very good time to begin a career as a forger.

A forger who could reproduce legal documents could make a lot of money. And not end up in the regent's jail—well, not if he was careful. Weasel had been careless only once in his whole criminal career—the day he'd decided to pick the pocket of an absentminded-looking elderly man and found he'd caught a justice. Or rather, a justice had caught him.

He could have been imprisoned then. He could even have been hanged. . . .

Weasel shivered. Pettibone would see them all hang.

Think your hand will be steady enough to forge documents with a ghost breathing in your ear?

No, he had to try. He owed Justice Holis too much. If the justice hanged, Weasel would never be free of him. Prison would be better!

Though if Weasel went up against the regent, he might have a chance to test that theory. Pettibone would be merciless to men who tried to overthrow him. Unless . . .

Unless someone with *more* power stopped him.

That might work! If Prince Edoran could be persuaded to oppose the regent, Weasel wouldn't have to do anything. He had never been present when Justice Holis spoke to the prince, but he knew there had been many such occasions. Holis had written to his fellow conspirators that he'd begun to earn the prince's trust. He wouldn't have said that if he wasn't certain. Had he earned enough trust, enough royal favor, that the prince would override the regent?

He'd better have, Weasel thought grimly, as the small troop of guards reached a corner and passed out of sight.

There were only two ways to get the justice out of this. One was a royal pardon, the other was a jailbreak. And a jailbreak meant overpowering the palace guards, which would require an army, which Weasel didn't have.

He was going to pay a call on the prince.

CHAPTER 2

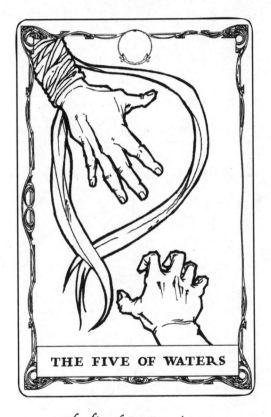

THE FIVE OF WATERS

The Five of Waters: mistrust.

Help may be found in unexpected places, or a source of aid relied upon may fail.

2

The palace was well guarded. The stables were guarded. Even the kitchens were guarded. But the laundry where the servants' clothes were washed was not only unguarded, it was closed with a lock so cheap that Weasel picked it almost as fast as he could have opened it with a key.

He'd gone back to Justice Holis' house to retrieve his shoes, his own warm coat, and the lock picks that the justice didn't know he'd kept. He'd hesitated over the well-honed knives in the kitchen. But when you planned to trick your way into the presence of royalty to ask a favor, coming armed might not be the best idea. Besides, Weasel preferred to use his wits.

He hadn't had to break into the justice's house, for Holis had showed him the crack in the back wall where he kept a spare key. In case Weasel lost his, he'd said. As if giving any key to a boy who'd picked his pocket only a few days before hadn't been an act of insanity in the first place. Or was it? That had been the moment when not disappointing the justice had begun to matter.

Inside the laundry Weasel closed the door behind him, holding still while his eyes adapted to the dim light that came from a well-banked fire under a great copper kettle. Weasel wasn't certain what kind of clothing a palace servant wore, but surely there would be more footmen's garb than anything else. In fact, a close inspection indicated that there were more stable hands and gardeners than footmen, and quite a few cooks. But of the fancy outfits, there were far more of the cream-colored britches, with the slightly darker coats and green waistcoats, so that was probably what footmen wore.

Weasel was thin, and small for his fourteen years, so it took a while to find clothes that fit him. With any luck, the buckled leather shoes Justice Holis had thought appropriate for a junior clerk would pass for a footman as well. He had no idea how they wore their hair. Justice Holis bound his graying locks in a queue at the back of his neck, as the noblemen did. But Weasel's hair, from long habit more than faith, was cut short in the fashion favored by followers of the One God. Most townsmen worshipped the One God, and surely at least some of the palace footmen were hired from their ranks. He hoped.

This would be dangerous—no question about it. He could still walk away. . . . But could he run far enough to escape the memory of his debt? No, he had to try.

The sky was going gray with the coming dawn when Weasel let himself out of the laundry and set off toward the palace's rear gate.

He'd been there several times, on errands for the justice, but he'd never gone past the gate or dealt with anyone more highly ranked than the guards who were posted there.

It seemed he'd timed his arrival well. As he turned down the street toward the gate, he saw a group of footmen and maids ahead of him, wearing clothes just like the ones he'd stolen.

Weasel picked up his pace and managed to catch up with the yawning young maid who brought up the rear.

"Good morning. I'm We-William. William Stebbing. I was introduced to so many people yesterday that I've forgotten half of them, but I don't think we met. In fact," he finished, ogling her with exaggerated admiration, "I'm sure we didn't meet. I'd have remembered *you*."

She giggled, as he'd hoped she would. "Your first day?"

"Second," Weasel told her. "And I hope I can keep a few more of the details in my head today. I served someone from the wrong side yesterday, and I swear"—Who supervised footmen? A steward? An over-footman?—"the old man practically had a stroke."

Weasel didn't know much about footmen, but he did know that they served at dinner, and that there was a right side to serve from. He hoped no one would ask him what it was.

The girl shrugged. "Well, it's the palace, see? Master Gerand insists on everything just so. I'm Mabby, by the way. Mabby Hickman."

A city name, a city accent, and most of the footmen around him wore their hair cut city short. The bad news was that their shoes were black with silver buckles, not brown with brass. The good news was that no one looked at his shoes as he passed through the gate, chatting easily with Mabby.

Once through the gate, they crossed a small yard. An ordinary-looking door led to a plain hallway, where the maids promptly began heading through a door on the right, and the footmen went on. Where were they going? Weasel's steps slowed. He couldn't ask without making Mabby suspicious, but she put her own interpretation on his reluctance.

"It's just inspection and handing out tasks," she said. "Master Gerand won't bite. And you look . . . " Her gaze swept over him and stopped on his shoes.

"What are you wearing those for?"

Weasel sighed. "The black ones pinched. They rubbed blisters on my toes. These are my best. I thought maybe they'd do."

"They won't," said Mabby. "But Master Gerand can find you tasks in the servants' hall until the cobbler can fit you better."

Judging by her sympathetic expression, working in the servants' hall was a step down, so Weasel sighed. "No use putting it off, I suppose. If I'm in the hall, perhaps I'll see you later."

"Perhaps you will," she said, with a saucy smile.

She went through the door along with the rest of the maids, and Weasel followed the footmen . . . and then walked casually past the door where they all entered, continuing straight to the end of the hall, where another plain door opened into the largest, busiest kitchen Weasel had ever seen.

It was just after sunrise, but there had to be over forty people chopping things, mixing things, and dashing about. The thought of trying to carry up the prince's breakfast tray crossed Weasel's mind, odds were that Prince Edoran slept till near noon. Weasel needed to hide himself in the palace, or find some task to look busy and invisible at, until the prince dragged his lazy arse out of bed.

He spotted a door on the other side of the kitchen and set off briskly, like a man with an errand to perform. The cooks and their helpers were far too occupied to notice him, much less his shoes— though he was almost run down by a girl carrying a basket of apples that was nearly as big as she was. He passed through the kitchen door and strode down another utilitarian hall.

Weasel was beginning to think that the rumors about palace splendor were exaggerated, until he passed through yet another door and into the dining room.

It was empty, which was probably a good thing, for Weasel didn't think he could have controlled his expression.

Gold glittered everywhere, from the tassels on the drapes, to the gilding on the ornamental plaster on the ceiling, to the dishes displayed in a cabinet, behind panes of clear glass.

It wasn't quite as gloriously filchable as it looked, he told himself firmly. The gold leaf that seemed to decorate every surface would probably be so thin it would only make up a handful of gold blessings if it were melted and cast into coin. The tableware that went with the dishes, which might be solid gold, was doubtless locked in a strongbox somewhere.

It was the richest room Weasel had ever seen, and he had to shake off the spell of all that glitter before he could go on.

The hallway that opened off the dining room was less fancy, though the polished wood and thick rugs, the huge oil paintings of folk in silk and jewels, still made Weasel feel like he was walking in a dream.

A well-dressed older man turned the corner and came toward him. But when he saw Weasel, his face registered no more awareness than it did when he looked at the furniture. This was how Weasel had thought all the rich behaved, until he met Justice Holis. Stepping aside with lowered eyes as the man passed, Weasel was delighted to be invisible right now. It wasn't the inhabitants of the palace he had to fear, but those who worked here. A nobleman would look at him and see nothing but a footman, about some errand, no doubt. A footman would see a stranger, idle, where he had no business being. Weasel needed a task.

But it wasn't till he wandered into the front hall and saw several dozen letters lying on a stand that inspiration came to him.

He pulled one from the middle of the pile, so whoever had put them there wouldn't notice anything amiss. There was a small silver tray under a flower vase—where had they gotten fresh flowers this time of year? But the vase looked just as good sitting on the table without it.

Weasel laid the letter in the exact center of the tray and carried it off. Now, if anyone stopped him he had the perfect excuse—an urgent message for the prince. *Do you know if he's awake yet? No? Then I'd better wait, don't you think? When would be the best time to deliver it? Where will His Highness be then?*

This was perfect! It would take him right into the prince's presence.

The prince's bedroom was probably somewhere above the ground floor, so Weasel climbed the sweeping staircase. As he walked down one of the long corridors, a footman emerged from one of the doors carrying a coal scuttle and a hearth brush.

Weasel hesitated. His original thought had been to avoid his fellow servants, but now . . .

"I've got a message here for the prince," he said. "Do you know if he's awake yet?"

The footman snorted. "Of course he's awake. A regular rooster, he is."

Weasel felt his brows rise, at the man's contemptuous tone as much as his own surprise that the prince was awake this early.

"Do you know where I can find him?"

"They took his breakfast tray in not fifteen minutes ago," said the man, gesturing down the corridor with his brush. "So he's probably still in his suite."

"Thank you." Weasel walked in the direction the man had indicated. He'd expected to have hours to prepare for this conversation. Hours to learn the layout of the corridors, plan an escape route.

It was good that he would reach the prince sooner, he told himself. Less chance of getting caught. And what he needed to say wasn't going to change, no matter how many times he rehearsed it.

Once they came in sight, there was no doubt which doors led to the prince's room. No, suite. The double doors at the end of the corridor were painted white and decorated with twining vines that were covered with yet more gold leaf.

Weasel took a steadying breath and tapped softly on one door. It was opened by a man in a tight black coat, who Weasel thought must be the prince's valet. He looked like a valet, with his narrow, fussy face and thin lips.

The lips parted. "Your business?" The man frowned. "I don't know you."

"I'm new," said Weasel. The nervous quaver in his voice would be natural in a new footman, right? "It's just my second day, but there was no one else in the hall when it came. A message for the prince," he added, lifting the tray.

Would the valet take the letter in? What could Weasel do if—

But the man stood aside and beckoned for him to enter the spacious sitting room. It was, of course, very rich, but Weasel was almost accustomed to gilt by now, and he had no time to gawk. The valet, hissing exasperation, corrected Weasel's grip on the tray from two-handed, secure, and comfortable to one-handed, uncomfortable, and precarious. It was probably incredibly elegant, but . . .

It was too late to complain, even to himself, about the absurdity of formal manners. The valet opened another door.

Weasel had a vague impression that the royal bedroom, its velvet drapes open to admit the morning light, wasn't as glittery as he'd expected, but most of his attention was fixed on its occupant.

Prince Edoran was sitting up, propped by a mountain of pillows, eating toast from a tray and reading a slim volume that might have been poetry. He looked small, but that could be because he was alone in a bed that would have held four without crowding. His hair, long enough to fall past his thin collarbones, was a nondescript brown.

The valet's hand on his shoulder urged Weasel forward.

"You've an urgent message here, Your Highness," the valet said. "Can it be you've acquired an admirer I don't know about?"

The prince laid his book aside, his brows drawing down in a scowl. "If I have, it's none of your business."

The valet was too close for Weasel to risk a whisper. He held out the tray, trying to catch the prince's eye, but it seemed Prince

Edoran was one of those noblemen who thought that servants were furniture. He paid no attention to Weasel as he picked up the letter, broke the seal, and opened it.

His eyes widened. His gaze turned to Weasel, sweeping up and down, lingering a moment on his shoes. "Is there a verbal message that accompanies this?"

"Yes, Your Highness," said Weasel gratefully.

"Very well." He turned to the valet. "You may go."

"But Your Highness, surely you'll need—"

"I command it," the prince said firmly.

"Ah, a female admirer," said the valet, with a coy smirk. He bowed and backed out of the room, closing the door behind him.

The prince's eyes settled on Weasel, brown and intent. "If the tailor sent you to whisper sweet nothings in my ear along with his bill, I'm going to be very surprised."

"Sorry," said Weasel. "I got it out of a pile on the stand at the foot of the stairs."

"Unsorted mail," said the prince. "Who are you?"

"I'm Justice Holis' clerk," said Weasel, relief flooding his veins. He would be able to deliver his news, convince this foppish prince—

"Ah," said the prince. "So he sent you to whisper in my ear. That makes more sense than the tailor."

"He didn't send me to . . . I mean, he didn't send me at all," Weasel told him. "I came to tell you that he needs your help. Desperately. He's been arrested."

Bewilderment crossed the prince's face. Weasel had a feeling it was the first honest expression he'd seen there. "Holis is a justice. How could he be arrested?"

"He was arrested by the palace guard," said Weasel grimly. "The palace guard and Regent Pettibone's clerk."

The prince's expression came back under his control, as abruptly as a slamming door. "What was the charge?"

"They didn't say," said Weasel. "But I'm guessing it will be treason. You'll have to pardon him. A royal pardon is the only thing that can get him out of that charge."

"A pardon is only necessary for the guilty," said the prince. "Should I assume from your request that there's plenty of evidence to convict him?" His voice was casual, almost flippant, and Weasel gritted his teeth.

"No, what they were planning was legal. Well, sort of. And they were never plotting against you, anyway. They were plotting against Regent Pettibone!"

"Then they're in trouble," said Prince Edoran. "Because Pettibone has legal authority over Deorthas till I turn twenty-two, and I doubt even the best lawyers will be able to drag out a trial for that long."

He lifted his teacup and started to sip, but it was empty. He frowned and reached for the pot, but Weasel picked up the tray, holding it out of his reach.

"Justice Holis said you knew him! He said he'd earned your trust!"

"Yes, well, that was foolish of me, wasn't it?" The prince

should have looked foolish, sitting in bed holding the dainty, empty cup. Weasel had never seen such a bleak expression in his life. "Since he was evidently using me, to plot against—"

The door opened. Weasel jumped so hard the dishes on the tray rattled.

The man who entered was short, probably not much taller than Weasel in his stocking feet, but the heels on his shoes were at least three inches high. He wore a brocaded dressing gown over a nightshirt that bore more lace than the prince's did. His long hair had been neatly combed back and bound at the nape of his neck, and he carried a slender cane. It didn't seem to go with the dressing gown, but Weasel supposed it must be fashionable, for he never leaned on it.

Three guards followed the nobleman into the room.

"Seize the imposter," the man told them calmly. "Good morning, Your Highness. I must apologize—"

The rest of his apology was lost in the crash of crockery when Weasel flung the tray at the guards and ran. They were between him and the door, but if he could open a window . . . if the ground below was soft . . .

He had one leg over the sill when they dragged him back into the room. He struggled, stupidly, uselessly, until they cuffed him so hard that bright lights flashed across his vision and he sank to his knees.

His hearing returned before his sight.

". . . as I saw his shoes, I knew he was an imposter," the valet was saying. "So of course, I went immediately to the regent."

"Of course," the prince said dryly.

"I'd not intended to trouble you with this distressing news before you rose, Your Highness," said the man, who must be Regent Pettibone. "But it seems a group of nobles, justices, and a few naval officers have been plotting to assassinate you and place another on the throne."

"Tha's not true," said Weasel. The left side of his face throbbed and his tongue felt stiff and clumsy. But if he didn't speak now, he would never get another chance. "They were plotting 'gainst the regent. Not against you." He focused his wavering vision on the prince, who was still sitting in bed, looking remarkably unruffled. The justice had *cared* about this indifferent brat. Clearly, one of his few mistakes.

"Even this boy, who you tell us belongs to Holis, admits they were plotting," said Pettibone swiftly. "Perhaps he has forged some kind of evidence—"

"No!" Weasel exclaimed. He wished he'd thought of it.

"No," the prince confirmed. "He came to me with nothing but his word." There was an odd note in his voice. Pettibone caught it too.

"I have evidence of the conspirators' guilt. Not only sworn testimony, but documents seized during the arrests."

"How many arrests?" the prince asked.

"Your pardon?"

"How many were involved in this plot?"

"Eighteen that we've discovered so far, six of them ring leaders, with your cousin, Shareholder Marchington, in command of the scheme. He was the one they planned to place on the throne—since he was, at least, of the true line. Though not, of course, the true king."

"No," said Edoran grimly. "That would be me. Since you used to be a justice yourself, Pettibone, I'm sure your evidence is sound. But with all the unrest people keep telling me about, I think we'd better make sure the trials these men receive are open to the public and scrupulously fair."

Pettibone frowned. "In times of unrest, a show of strength is more likely to effect the desired result than a show of law."

"Won't we be showing sufficient strength if we hang them after they're convicted?" the prince asked.

"Your Highness . . . " Pettibone paused. His expression held only grave sorrow, but Weasel had seen enough people lie with their faces to read the determination beneath. "Your Highness, I must tell you that, due to the horrific nature of Shareholder Marchington's intentions and the civil disturbances of which we've been speaking, I felt an immediate display of royal authority was both necessary and desirable."

Weasel frowned, trying to sort through this with his sluggish wits, but the prince beat him to it.

"You hanged him."

Weasel cried out in protest and then felt foolish, for he knew nothing of this Marchington. Still, something in him despaired at the news.

"I thought it necessary, Your Highness," said Pettibone, in an apologetic tone that didn't fool anyone. "His guilt was clear. I can show you the evidence, if you wish, but much of it is accounts and other such tedious stuff."

"I see." The prince's composed face was pale. "But I'm not the one who should see that evidence. Have you hanged any of the others?"

Weasel's heart contracted, but Pettibone was already shaking his head.

"Not yet, but their executions are scheduled as soon as the evidence can be sifted and presented to you. Unless, of course, you want me to take that burden. . . . "

"No," said the prince. He straightened his spine and stared at the regent. "Neither you nor I will judge those men. They will be tried by a panel of justices, in open court."

Pettibone sighed. "Your Highness, several of the traitors *are* justices. If there are more, whom we haven't uncovered . . . "

"They will be tried in open court." Edoran swallowed, then took a deep breath. "I command it."

The regent shook his head. "This has been a shock to you."

"Not that much of a shock," said the prince. "A trial in open court, starting one month from today. That will give you time to gather all the evidence you'll need, won't it?"

He meant, forge the evidence you'll need. Weasel's blood chilled. The prince knew! He knew what the regent was doing. He was trying to buy time.

"Most of the evidence has already been gathered," Pettibone told him coolly. "Three days is sufficient to set it in order and select a panel. A month gives an appearance of hesitation, of weakness, on the part of the crown."

"And three days gives an appearance of haste," said the prince. "Three weeks. I *command* this."

Pettibone hesitated a moment more. "If Your Highness insists, I have no choice but to yield. Two weeks, and then the trial commences. I shall announce it."

He bowed to the scowling prince and gestured to the guards, who hauled Weasel to his feet and then toward the door.

"You said three weeks," Weasel cried to the prince. "Stop him!"

His feet scrabbled for purchase on the polished floor, and one of the guards cuffed him hard enough to make his head ring.

The prince's gaze fell to his hands, clenched around the empty cup.

"You know what he is!" Weasel shouted. "You withless piece of sludge! S*top* him!"

The guards dragged him from the room and the regent followed, closing the door behind him.

Two weeks! What could he do in two weeks? Even if the justices Pettibone selected were impartial, and they wouldn't be, how could he—

"What do you want us to do with the boy?" a guardsman asked the regent.

"Lock him up with the others," said Pettibone. "We'll try him along with his master."

They passed out of the suite and into the hallway. There was no one in sight; no wandering noble, not even a maid he could ask to contact one of Holis' friends.

"There's no room in the old cells, sir," the guard protested. "What with the traitors, and their families, and their clerks and such, they're packed in like salt fish. If you'd just let us use the town lockup . . . "

"No," Pettibone snapped. "They're traitors to the crown. They stay in the palace dungeons, under palace guard."

Lest they succeed in getting some rumor out into the world that they were innocent, Weasel realized. In the palace, Pettibone had complete control over who the prisoners saw and spoke to. Even the servants who took away the slop pails would be his men.

"If you say so, sir," said the guard. "But I'm telling you, there's no room."

The regent's frown faded. "Then put him in the storeroom with that other young nuisance. It won't matter what he tells her, for she'll be in no position to act on it."

"That'll do," said the guard. "Thank—"

The footman with the coal scuttle came out of a door at the other end of the passage. It was a slim chance, but he might not get another.

"Help me!" Weasel screamed at the top of his lungs.

The footman turned and stared.

"I'm innocent! Tell Justice Danvers! Tell Justice Witworth! Tell—"

The guard's fist crashed down.

CHAPTER 3

THE EIGHT OF FIRES

The Eight of Fires: imprisonment.
Being forced into a particular set of circumstances, or course of action.
Or possibly, imprisonment.

3

"Are you really unconscious?" a girl's voice asked.

In fact, Weasel had never quite lost consciousness, though he'd had little control over his stumbling feet. The guards had dragged him through what felt like miles of corridor, and up and down flights of stairs, before dropping him here on the floor. Wherever here was.

Considering the way his head ached, Weasel had thought it prudent to stay limp and keep his eyes closed until he heard them close the door and lock it behind them. Then it seemed prudent to feign helplessness, until he knew more about the source of the light footsteps that slowly approached him after the guards had gone—especially since he wasn't so sure his helplessness was feigned.

But a girl didn't sound like much of a threat, so Weasel opened his eyes and promptly wished he hadn't. The small square of sunlight lancing through the barred window made his headache explode. He rolled onto his side and clutched his stomach. "I think I'm going to be sick."

"Please don't," said the girl sincerely. "The slop pot smells bad enough as it is. Take deep breaths."

Weasel followed her advice and found that his stomach slowly settled and his muscles relaxed. He would have to get up in a minute, confront the girl, and find some way out of this place.

Whatever it was. Any minute now. He was still thinking that, when he fell asleep.

The next awakening was better than the first. His left eye throbbed dully, but the worst of the headache had passed and his stomach had settled. A damp cloth lay across the sore side of his face and a rolled blanket had been tucked under his head, which was nice because the stone floor on which he lay was cold, and very hard. Weasel lifted the cloth and looked at it. A kerchief. The kind countrywomen wore over their hair, and countrymen sometimes tied around their necks.

"You going to stay awake this time?" the girl asked tartly, and Weasel turned.

She had probably worn it around her neck, he decided, for she was dressed as a boy. Countrywomen did that sometimes when engaged in rough work, though they usually dressed in proper skirts to come into the city.

She looked to be about his own age, and the orange light pouring through the window awoke red highlights in her long, dark hair. If her face had matched that chestnut hair she would have been beautiful, but her features were ordinary. A scattering of freckles crossed her nose.

Weasel was more interested in the fact that the light was orange and came through the window at a very low angle.

"How long did I sleep?" His voice was urgent, but he sat up slowly. His headache didn't worsen, so he rose carefully to his feet.

"All day." The girl watched him with critical interest, making no move to help. Weasel would have been annoyed, except . . .

"This yours?" He offered her the kerchief.

She took it and tied her hair into a thick ponytail.

"I'm Arisa," she said. "Arisa Benison."

The clothes were country but the accent wasn't. The name could have come from anywhere in Deorthas.

"Why'd they lock up a nice girl like you?" Weasel asked. He crossed to the window, still moving cautiously, but he felt steadier the longer he was on his feet.

"What's your name?" she asked. "And what's a nice clerk like you doing here?"

"How do you know I'm a clerk?" Weasel asked. The windowsill was above the level of his eyes. He stood on tiptoe and still saw nothing but the sky.

"You have to stand on the slop pot to see out," the girl said. Aside from a handful of blankets, it was the only object in the room. "And even then you can't see much. About your profession, you're dressed like a footman, but footmen don't have inky fingers. I took a guess. I was right, too," she finished smugly.

Weasel opened his mouth to ask how she knew that, then realized he'd confirmed it himself.

"Are you going to make me guess your name?" she added.

"It's Weasel," he said, dragging the big crockery pot from the corner where she'd tucked it. It was nearly a foot tall, and she was right about the smell.

"Your parents named you Weasel?" Her brows rose.

"My mother named me William. Weasel was the name that stuck."

"What about your father?"

"He died in an accident, a few months before I was born. He was a stevedore. He was helping unload a ship when one of the ropes holding a crate snapped. Killed three men—bam! Hold this steady for me, will you?"

"I'm sorry," said the girl, as she knelt and grasped the pot. "My father's dead too."

Weasel shrugged. "I never knew him."

Drawing himself up on the bars, he managed to get both feet balanced on the sturdy rim without tipping it over.

The stone wall was almost three feet thick, and the bars were set on the inner edge of the window. Even when he pulled himself up to the top, Weasel could see nothing but a square of distant waves. It looked like they were far below the cell, though from his angle it was hard to tell how far. It made sense, anyway, since the palace stood on a bluff that overlooked the sea.

Perhaps it was only imagination, but one of the bars seemed to shift as he lowered himself and stepped down.

"I'd have thought the dungeons would be belowground."

"I don't think we're in the dungeons," said Arisa. "When they put me in here, one of the guards said that the dungeons were full. There used to be shutters on this window." She pointed to holes in the wall, where hinges had been attached. "And I found a bit of grain on the floor, and some splinters that might have come from a crate. I think this was a storeroom, and they cleaned it out when they needed extra space for prisoners."

"Then why are there bars on the window?" Weasel asked.

"To keep the prisoners in?" Her expression was innocent, but sarcasm leaked into her voice, and Weasel grinned.

"I didn't say this was the first time they've kept prisoners here," the girl went on, more soberly. "But I think those bars were added after the room was built. They're set in mortar, not in the stone."

"Are they?" Weasel breathed. Bars set in stone, when the cell was built, were solid till the iron rusted through. Bars set in mortar lasted only as long as the mortar did. Parts of the palace were thousands of years old, and judging by the thickness of the wall, this room was one of them.

He reached up and wrapped both hands around one of the bars, trying to rotate it first one way, then the other. At least he didn't have to balance on the pot to grasp it.

"How long have you been here?" he asked the girl. She'd clearly had time to investigate the cell. The bar wasn't moving. He went on to the next.

"Day before yesterday. They bring bread and cheese in the morning and a bowl of bean porridge in the evening. They've already gone," she added, at his look of alarm. "Though why you care I don't know. I shook those bars. They're solid."

"Did you try twisting them?" The second bar didn't budge. Weasel went on to the third.

"Why would I want to twist—"

The third bar turned in Weasel's grasp, its mortar grating. His half-muffled whoop of joy made the girl stare as if he were a lunatic.

So Weasel explained, as he worked the bar back and forth, that loosened mortar acts like a grinding stone; that if you can turn the bar, eventually you can use it to file itself free.

When his arms tired, she took a turn, and he put the chamber pot to its accustomed use while she politely pretended not to notice.

As the bar moved more and more freely, a small hole formed around it. They started pulling it toward them as they twisted it, and slowly the round hole became an oval, then a short slot.

Digging idle hands into his pockets, Weasel discovered the knife he used to sharpen quills. The guards had evidently over-looked it, which wasn't as careless as it sounded, for the blade was less than an inch long. But after he found it, whichever of them wasn't working at the window cut their blankets into strips and then knotted them together. To Weasel's critical eye, it wasn't much of a rope; the knots seemed to take up most of the strip, and when he pulled on one section it stretched in a thoroughly ominous fashion. It gave him something to do when Arisa was twisting the bar, but he'd hate to trust that rope with his life.

Even with both of them working, it had been dark for several hours when the bar finally pulled free. Arisa, who had been turn-ing it, tumbled onto her backside, but she sprang up again imme-diately, her face alight with excitement.

"Forget the pot and stand on me!" she told him. "You're smaller than I am."

In fact, Weasel had already noticed that she was both taller and, as she worked the bar long past the point he'd have been exhausted, stronger than he was. It was spending the last three years writing legal documents that had made him so soft, Weasel told himself. But if she hadn't noticed that he was weaker, as well as smaller, he wasn't about to call it to her attention by defending himself. And besides, sometimes smaller was better!

She got down on her hands and knees, and Weasel stepped onto her back as if it were a footstool and squirmed through the new-made gap in the bars. He looked down.

"Rot!"

"What? What is it?" Arisa demanded.

"We're not even close to the ground. This window is over a hundred feet high!"

Possibly more. The moon had risen, and judging distance in the dark was always harder, but the ledge of rocks at the base of the wall was a long way down. A narrow ledge too. Just wide enough to smash your body before it bounced down the cliff into the sea, which was even farther below.

Down was suicide, even with their blanket rope. So what about up?

Weasel wiggled a few inches farther and turned to look. The nearest window opening was twenty feet above them. And with the luck he was having lately, even if they could have reached it, it was bound to be barred. But looking at the wall's sharp curve, he now knew where they were. He wiggled back through the window.

"We're in the old watchtower," he told Arisa, dropping to the floor as he spoke. He staggered, and she caught him. "It's on the far side of the oldest part of the palace. I thought this wing had been closed for decades."

Arisa clearly wasn't interested in palace architecture. "Can we climb down?"

"No," said Weasel. "The walls are sheer and we're way too high."

"Even with the rope? If we climb down a bit there might be cracks in the wall. Or something."

"Or there might not be," said Weasel. "In which case you're hanging on the end of a fraying rope, fifty feet above a rock ledge, beyond which is an even bigger drop. No, thank you."

Her mouth tightened stubbornly.

"You want to see for yourself?" Weasel asked.

"Yes."

Then he had to get down on his hands and knees, so she could step onto his back and haul herself onto the thick ledge. It was a bit insulting that she hadn't taken his word for it, but he wanted to examine the floor, anyway.

He was still crawling around several minutes later, when she dropped back into the room.

"You're right," she admitted. "I felt all around the window for cracks. There aren't many, and none of them are deep enough to support a climber. We're going to miss those blankets, though. What are you doing?"

"Checking out the floor," said Weasel, which should have been obvious, since his nose was almost pressed against it. "In prisons, real prisons, they build the floors so the stones can't be pried up. But this tower wasn't built to be a prison. And I'll bet the mortar around these flagstones is really, really old."

"You know a lot about prisons, for an honest clerk."

"I used to know a lot of burglars," Weasel told her. "Not really well, but there was a tavern where I'd eat sometimes, and a lot of them met there. They told stories about breaking into and out of all kinds of places."

"And they didn't slit your throat when they caught you listening?"

"I was in a different branch of the same trade," Weasel admitted. "At the time."

One of the stones shifted slightly under his probing hands.

The first stone he found that had enough give to rock was too big to lift. It took another hour of crawling around before they found another stone that wiggled. And it took most of another hour for Weasel to chip out the mortar around it with his penknife.

But neither of them was bored. This chance to escape was beginning to look like . . . well, a chance, and Weasel filled the time telling her about Justice Holis' arrest and his meeting with the prince.

"I've never heard of this Concordance of Nobles," the girl commented thoughtfully. "But it sounds like your friend's conspiracy came close to succeeding, and the regent won't take that lightly. Was Justice Holis one of the top conspirators?"

"One of them," Weasel confirmed grimly. "But I have two weeks to get him out. Well, thirteen days now." Could he possibly get the justice out in thirteen days? If he failed . . . Weasel pushed the thought aside; thinking of consequences of failure made his stomach knot. He'd be no use to the justice if he went into fits. He took a steadying breath. "I can't believe I slept all day."

"That's not uncommon, after a beating," Arisa told him. "Your body needs to recover from the shock."

"How would you know? You get beat up a lot?" It might have sounded sarcastic, but Weasel was honestly curious about this girl.

"Not me," she admitted. "But I've seen it. My mother's an . . . importer of sorts. It's a rough trade."

Weasel's brows rose. "Your mother's a smuggler?"

"Not herself," said Arisa. "She's a dressmaker, really. But she owns a warehouse where she keeps fabric, and since she's a dressmaker, people expect to find bolts of silk there. Do you have any idea how high the import duty on silk is?"

"Don't people also expect to see a duty-paid stamp on the bolt end?" Weasel asked.

"They do see duty-paid stamps," Arisa told him cheerfully. "My mother takes care of that. Sometimes the ink is even dry."

"Nice," said Weasel sincerely. "And of course, being a respectable widow—please tell me she's a respectable widow— no one would ever suspect her of dealing in smuggled goods."

"My mother is an entirely respectable widow, who'd faint at the mere thought of smuggled goods," said Arisa. "Unfortunately, some of her buyers here in the city aren't that respectable. I was with them, carrying a message from my mother, when we were all arrested."

"Ah."

"They don't know who my mother really is," she went on. "So I need to get out of here before the guards figure out that the only way to find my mother is through me. Do you want me to work on that for a while?"

"I think I've got it," Weasel told her. "Let's try to rock the stone."

It took a while to get a rhythm established, but soon the stone was bouncing a little higher with each push. Suddenly Arisa reversed her grip, slipping her fingers under the edge.

"It's heavy!"

"Here, let me get in there." Weasel scrambled around to her side of the stone. With both of them pushing, it tipped up easily, balancing on the stones beside it. The moonlight didn't penetrate the black pit that yawned beneath.

"This isn't good," said Weasel. "The floor could be twenty or thirty feet down. We need light."

"We don't have light," said Arisa. She fished in her pockets and pulled out a brass droplet.

"They didn't take your money?"

"They took my purse, not the coins in my pockets. But I don't have much."

She continued to search till she came up with a tin nothing. She held it over the center of the opening and dropped it. The soft clink sounded almost instantly.

"Not too far," she said.

"It could still be far enough to break an ankle," Weasel told her. "Particularly in the dark. And we don't even know what we'd land on."

A reckless grin transformed the girl's plain face. "One way to find out." She turned and slid her legs into the hole.

"Are you crazy?" Weasel demanded. "You don't know what's down there!"

"I know what's up here," said Arisa. Was her face paler? In the dim moonlight Weasel couldn't be sure, but her determined expression was clearly visible. "I'm tired of this place. Your company excepted, of course."

She lowered her body into the gap, catching herself first with her elbows, then with just her hands clutching the edge. Then she let go.

Thump. Crash. "Ow!"

"What? How far is it? What did you hit? Are you hurt?"

A soft snort emerged from the darkness, followed by a scraping sound. "Nice to know what your priorities are."

Weasel thought about what he'd said. "Sorry. Are you hurt?"

"No." She sounded more cheerful now. "Not beyond a few bruises. I hit a crate on the way down and it broke."

Shuffling sounds now.

"There are a lot of crates down here, and other stuff too. Wait a minute. I have an idea."

"What idea?"

"Give me a minute. I've found the wall now, and I'm feeling along it. . . . Yes!"

"What?"

He was answered by the rasp of a striker, and a glow of light that wavered and then steadied. To his dark-adapted eyes, the candlelight seemed bright.

"People often leave them by the door," said Arisa. "In rooms they don't use much. Though someone's been here relatively recently. These strikers have only been around for about ten years, and the candles don't have much dust on them."

"They're the only thing that doesn't." Weasel peered through the opening into a large room filled with stacked crates, and cloth-covered lumps that were probably old furniture. There were also chests, some of which could have been thrown up onto the roof of a coach tomorrow without anyone giving them a second look. But other chests, made of dark wood with iron hasps, had probably been here since the tower was built. There was even a pile of metal scraps Weasel thought was a suit of armor, but he couldn't be sure because all the pieces were lying in a heap on the floor. Everything was coated with dust.

"Can you move one of the bigger crates, so I can stand on it and reach the ceiling?" Weasel asked.

"It's not that long a drop." *You sissy,* her tone added.

"It's not the drop," Weasel told her. "This time I have an idea."

He took a small revenge, ignoring her questions while he tied the blanket rope to one of the secure bars and thrust the rest of it out the window. By the time he returned to the hole, a tall crate stood beneath it.

"Stand back," he warned her.

"Why?" But she stepped back, and the shower of loose mortar Weasel swept through the hole answered her question.

"All right," she said resignedly. "What are you doing?"

"Making it look like we're dead." As he lowered himself to the crate, he told her what he'd done.

"Do you really think they'll think we're dead?" She climbed

up to help him. Maneuvering the heavy flagstone from below was harder than lifting it in the first place.

"Depends. If they believe we've gone out the window and don't look farther, you bet they'll think we're dead. No one could survive that fall, and if we bounced off the ledge the sea would take the bodies. If they realize we weren't crazy enough to go out the window, they'll find this stone in about two minutes."

"So we'd better get out of here."

The stone thumped into place, bruising Weasel's knuckles. "Absolutely."

Only a minute later, they discovered that the door wouldn't open.

"You didn't check it?" Weasel asked incredulously.

"I was busy," said Arisa. She stood on her toes to look down through the door's small, barred vent. "I was getting the light you wanted, and stacking crates so you could get down, and helping you put the stone back for your fancy scheme."

"All right, all right. Can you see anything?"

"It's a padlock," said Arisa. When she took her face away from the vent, she had red marks on her forehead and chin. "I was hoping it would be a bolt, and we could reach down and slide it back."

"If I can reach it, I can pick it," said Weasel, trying to sound more confident than he felt.

Arisa eyed him dubiously. "I don't think you can. What about taking the hinges apart?"

"The hinges are on the other side."

"Oh. What about breaking it down? If we can find something heavy to use as a ram . . . "

"This door? Us and what other three men? These are oak planks, an inch thick. And looking at the spacing of the bolt heads, I'll bet they're braced with iron bands on the other side."

"I can't see the bands, but I could only see the lock because it stuck out from the door. And I don't think you can reach—"

"I can try," said Weasel.

It took several more minutes hauling crates around to build a platform where he could kneel to stretch his arm through the narrow gap. He had his lock picks laid out, ready, but . . .

"I can't reach it," Weasel gasped, straining again. "I can't even touch it, much less pick it."

"You couldn't . . . I don't know, reach down with a stick?"

"Maybe, but even if I could touch it with a stick, so what? I have to be able to reach it with my hand to pick the lock."

"Then we'd better start looking for a ram," said Arisa. Her face showed weary discouragement, but her voice was firm—the One God be thanked. The last thing Weasel needed was a weeping female.

And if his own eyes stung, well, that was because of the dust.

"A ram will make enough noise to fetch everyone in the tower," he objected.

"We haven't been making enough noise already? I don't think there's anyone else here. And even if someone does come, what do we have to lose? We're caught in this room as surely as we were in the cell."

That was true, but still . . . Weasel watched gloomily as she explored the shrouded furniture.

"One of these table legs might do, if we could break it off."

Weasel looked at the table in question. It appeared to consist of whole tree trunks, which had been bolted together and only then planed flat and polished. "You've got as much chance of breaking that table as you do the door. You'd need an ax."

"Maybe we can find one. They've got everything else down here. The armor! There might be an ax with it! Or a mace, or . . . " A sudden surge of hope carried Weasel across the room with her, to the corner where the discarded armor had been piled. It took several minutes to sort through it all, but in the end . . .

"Nothing." The girl's voice was still steady, but she wiped her cheeks with both hands, leaving dark smudges behind.

She was crying now, but Weasel wasn't about to complain. He felt like he might start any second himself.

"Look at the bright side," he said. "At least the air is fresh. When we hear them above us we can pound on the ceiling, and they'll lock us up in a real cell that we can't get out of. And feed us before they hang us."

"You call that the bright side?"

"Well, at least the air is . . ."

It struck both of them at the same moment. They stared at the candle.

"Why is the smoke flowing away from the door?" Arisa whispered.

"Because there's another way out! And we're going to find it!"

Without the stream of smoke showing the way, they'd never have looked for another door. But when they dragged away several chests, a large wardrobe cupboard, and a wooden statue of a man in old-fashioned clothes, there it was. An ordinary wooden door, set neatly into the stone wall.

"The hinges are on our side!" Weasel exclaimed. "Even if it's locked, we can—"

Arisa reached out and pulled the handle. Rust squealed as the door swung toward them.

"I hope you're right about us being the only ones here," said Weasel, stepping into the room. It was larger than the first, full of still more crates, chests, and odd-shaped lumps of fabric, as dusty as the last set.

"It's just another storeroom," Arisa said.

"But the candle smoke's still being pulled away." Weasel pointed to a corner.

There was barely room to thread their way between the stacks of palace detritus. Weasel gave wide berth to a heap of old curtains, which had to be full of mice, and maybe rats. Arisa sneezed twice.

When they reached the far wall, the smoke rose upward. Arisa held her candle over her head. "There's a hatch up there, or something," she said. "I can barely see it."

Weasel frowned. The ceiling here was much taller than in the previous rooms—almost three stories. "How do we get up there? That hatch is higher than the floor of our old cell. Suppose . . . " His heart sank. "Suppose it just leads out to the sea, like the window did." A ventilation shaft. It seemed horribly likely.

"We're going in the opposite direction from the window," Arisa objected. "Look at the stubs of those beams, coming out of the wall. I think there was a floor up there once, and it burned or fell down. I think we're moving back toward the palace. I bet it's a secret passage."

Weasel laughed. "Secret passages only exist in three-volume novels," he told her. "Bad ones. But it must go somewhere, and to quote this girl I know, 'There's only one way to find out.'"

It was easy to find crates they could drag over to the wall below the hatch. It was harder finding chests and bits of furniture light enough to lift to the top of their growing stack.

Weasel was sorting through a corner, cluttered with what looked like the remains of a theatrical performance. At least, he couldn't think of anything else that called for an eight-foot-tall silhouette of a tree. Some of the chests here, which probably held costumes, were lighter. He reached into a bundle of filthy cloth, ready to yank his hands back at the first brush of a furry body, and his fingertips touched metal.

A sudden surge of dizziness brought him to his knees, his vision graying away. His grip on the object tightened instinctively—it helped hold him up. When his senses cleared, his cheek was pressed against the dirty cloth and Arisa was frowning down at him.

"Are you all right?"

"I guess so," said Weasel cautiously. The strange weakness was passing as rapidly as it had come on. "I just got dizzy. I haven't eaten since . . . it must be day before yesterday by now. You should have saved me some food."

"I tried," said Arisa. "The guards took it when they came for the dishes. What's that?"

"A shield," said Weasel, and then wondered why he was so certain, for fabric obscured its shape. He fumbled the cloth aside. It was a shield, steel plate over dark wood, with rotting leather straps. It looked old, and battered, and real—a better match to the dismantled armor in the first room than to the silver-painted swords of the theater.

Arisa's expression brightened. "I wonder if there's a weapon to go with it?"

"We don't need an ax or a mace now," Weasel pointed out. "We need a ladder."

"I was hoping for a knife."

"I've got a knife," said Weasel.

"A *real* knife."

"What would you do with a knife?" Weasel asked.

Something in the girl's smile made the fine hairs on his neck prickle.

There were no weapons to go with the shield, but buried under a pile of old backdrops, painted with rooms and forests and streets, Weasel did find a ladder, almost seven feet tall.

"It looks old," said Arisa dubiously. "Old and rotten."

"We'll test it before we put it on top of our stack," Weasel assured her.

It creaked unnervingly but held his weight, and when Arisa followed, it held hers, too. They wrestled it up on top of their pile of crates and chests and eyed the result warily, but there was no other choice.

The whole stack wobbled as Weasel scaled the ladder, even with Arisa holding its base, and at the top he had to dig out his lock picks to open the small, square hatch.

The small, square passage it opened onto was dark, smelling of wet stone and mold. Weasel scrambled in and held the top of the ladder as Arisa climbed up to join him. He'd never seen a broader grin.

"We're not out yet," he warned her. "It could just be a ventilation shaft. Or an old laundry chute."

"So? If it's an air vent it will lead to the outside, and maybe we can climb down from there. And if it's a laundry chute it will lead to the old laundry, and we can escape that way. Let's go!"

It wasn't a laundry chute, and if it was an air vent it was the oddest Weasel had ever encountered. They had to crawl on their hands and knees for almost twenty feet, and then the square passage changed to a tall slot, so narrow they had to turn sideways in places.

"I'll bet we're inside one of the walls," Arisa murmured.

According to Weasel's burglar friends, secret passages were the stuff of bad novels, but soon Weasel had to admit that it looked like one of the ancient kings had been a bad novel fan. After a time the passage changed again, the ceiling dropping so low that they had to walk bent over, though they didn't have to crawl. They climbed down a steep flight of stairs, followed by another narrow tunnel that soon widened into one so large they could walk upright, side by side.

This passage smelled more of damp earth than stone and mold, and even Weasel wasn't surprised when they came to another door.

"I don't believe it," he said. "A simple bolt. On *our* side."

"Don't be ridiculous," Arisa said. "If it's an escape passage they'd need to be able to get out, and keep people outside from coming in. A bolt makes perfect sense."

She pulled it back and pushed on the door. It didn't budge.

"I told you," said Weasel, with morose satisfaction. "It couldn't be that easy."

Arisa glared and shoved the door with all her strength. It opened about two inches.

It took both of them, pushing repeatedly, to force back the soil that had accumulated on the doorsill and tear the trailing vines, but soon the gap was big enough to step through.

"Outside!" Arisa whispered. "We've escaped!"

"Not entirely," said Weasel, looking at the back of the three huge marble statues that stood before them. "I recognize these."

"It's one of the old kings, with the sword and shield beside him." Arisa struggled through the underbrush behind the statue of a man who stood at the king's left, holding his sword. "They're in almost every town square."

After a moment's hesitation, Weasel picked up a stone and wedged the door open, just a few inches. You never knew when you'd need a bolt-hole, and the vines that trailed down the cliff behind the statues still concealed the door.

"We've got statues like this in the old parts of the city, as well," said Weasel. Was she a country girl after all? "But this set is inside the royal park, which is attached to the palace."

Arisa's mouth drooped in dismay. "Then we're still on the palace grounds?"

"Yes, but the good news is that there are half a dozen places you can climb over those walls—this was one of my favorite places to elude . . . well, anyone. We'll be out of here and into the city alleys in ten minutes. Or less. And then . . . "

"What will you do now?" Arisa asked curiously. "I'm going home, though I don't have to hurry. My mother won't expect me for another week. Will you try to reach the conspirators? If they had contacts in the army, maybe the army could break your justice out. Or maybe the conspirators could get him a lawyer?"

"A lawyer can't help him," said Weasel. "Not against Regent Pettibone. And the lord commander of the army is Regent Pettibone's man."

There had been some discussion of that in the letters Weasel copied, and Justice Holis had once hinted that the title of lord commander and actual command of the army were two different things. But hinting was all he'd done, and despite his jests about identifiable handwriting, Holis had written and copied the most important letters himself. Weasel didn't even know the identity of all the conspirators—but most of them were now in Pettibone's dungeon, so that hardly mattered.

"The conspiracy's finished," he went on aloud. "Even the prince couldn't—or at least he wouldn't—stand up to Pettibone. I need another kind of help. And food, and a safe place to stay for the rest of the night. And the justice would want me to pass on a warning, if there's still time.

"I'm going to church."

CHAPTER 4

THE ONE OF STARS

The One of Stars: the shrine.

The proper worship of any god, or holiness in day-to-day life.

4

It was the scent that Weasel remembered, as he opened the big church door; wet wool, stale sweat, and the big pot of soup that was set to simmering every evening in the kitchen behind the One God's shrine. When all the house owners in the neighborhood were locking up for the night, the church of the One God opened its doors, so that those who had no home might sleep safe, and those who hadn't eaten might be fed.

Weasel had taken advantage of both services in the lean time after his mother died, before he mastered his new trade. The benches were uncomfortable, but the soup wasn't bad.

He'd gone halfway down the aisle before he realized that Arisa had stopped at the threshold, peering warily inside. Definitely a country girl, despite the lack of accent. But she'd helped him break out of the cell, so he owed her a safe place to spend the night at least. He went back to the door, but she spoke before he could.

"There are people in there. Snoring. I can hear them."

"They're just poor," Weasel told her tartly. "It's not contagious." He took her arm and pulled her into the church.

Her gaze darted about, half-curious, half-nervous.

"They don't have anywhere else to sleep dry," Weasel continued. "Or some just need a meal."

"But how can the priest give his talk with all these people living here?"

"They don't live here. They'll be wakened at dawn and be gone an hour after. That's part of the deal. Then, except on Mansday when the priest gives his talk, the children come in for school. The ones too young to work, at least. Some stop coming when they're nine years old."

"That's still too young to work," said Arisa. "Did you go to school here?" She was walking so quietly her shoes hardly made a sound on the stone floor, though Weasel knew from past experience that it would take a shout or a crash to rouse most of the sleepers.

"Are you a . . . a follower?" she added.

Weasel had been in churches of the One God, for various purposes, throughout his life. But for some reason her question brought his earliest memories of the church flooding back; cold stone walls, hard benches, and an old man talking on and on while his mother hissed at him to *sit still!*

"I did go to school," he admitted. "Not in this church, but in one a lot like it. It was because I was literate that Justice Holis made me his clerk. As for being a follower . . . The One God didn't save either of my parents, so I don't figure I owe him."

Arisa nodded and didn't look shocked, the way most people did when Weasel told them that. Justice Holis hadn't been shocked either.

"The priest here, Father Adan, is a friend of the justice's," Weasel went on, leading her behind the shrine where the door to the kitchen was concealed.

"A friend?" Arisa asked. "Or . . . "

"Yes," Weasel told her. "The condordance didn't just need a

majority of the nobles, it needed the support of the church leaders as well. In fact, according to the old law, they were the ones who had to call for the meeting."

"How odd," said Arisa softly.

Weasel stirred the soup before taking two bowls from the stack beside the hearth. "What's odd?"

"If that law's as old as you say, the church leaders would have been . . . Never mind. It doesn't matter, and I'm hungry."

Arisa held the bowls while he ladled in soup. It was beef and barley tonight, and it wasn't bad, Weasel decided, chewing the first mouthful. Though as hungry as he was, he hardly cared what it tasted like. He ate half the bowl standing beside the hearth. Then he added another ladleful and kept eating while he climbed the stair that led to Father Adan's private quarters.

He was prepared to wake the priest. Warning him that most of his coconspirators had been arrested was more important than sleep. But when Weasel and Arisa reached the landing at the top of the stairs, light glowed beneath all three doors, and muffled sounds of movement came from the study.

"He already knows," said Arisa softly.

Weasel nodded and knocked. The sounds ceased. Weasel waited for several seconds before he realized that a knock on the door a few hours before dawn might alarm Father Adan right now.

"It's me, Weasel," he called. "Justice Holis' clerk."

The door opened and Father Adan appeared, blinking behind his spectacles. He was young for a priest, with brown hair already receding from his forehead. But the owlish eyes gazed at Weasel with sincere joy. "I heard that you were arrested with him."

He gestured for Weasel to enter, then stopped, staring at Arisa.

"I was, but we broke out of the palace. Not the justice," Weasel added swiftly, as incredulous delight dawned on the priest's face. "Just me and Arisa here."

Father Adan sighed. "I suppose that was too much to hope for. Come in, Mistress Arisa. You clearly know everything already."

Weasel stared at the chaotic study. He'd been here before, carrying messages from the justice. The room was always untidy, but now it looked like a whirlwind had struck it. "You're packing."

"And burning every paper that so much as mentions another man's name, whether he was involved with us or not," Father Adan confirmed. "There's a hunt shaping up. I'd hate to involve some innocent person, whose only crime was to have business with me or with the church. The regent's been concentrating on the nobles, but according to the old law the church *had* to be a part of the concordance. He'll be coming for us soon."

"But you're not a church leader," said Weasel. "They probably don't know about you."

"They may not know about me yet," said Father Adan. "But I can't depend on that to last. I've an old friend in . . . another city. I think it's time to pay him a visit."

Weasel saw that instead of the archaic, dark robes he usually wore, Father Adan was dressed in brown britches and a plain waistcoat. The matching brown coat was thrown over a chair. With his thick spectacles, he looked like an accountant.

"A braver man might stay," the priest went on. "Might join his friends, stand up for his convictions. But—"

"That would be stupid," said Weasel bluntly.

"That's the conclusion I reached," Father Adan admitted. "That, or perhaps I'm not the stuff of which martyrs are made."

Weasel snorted. "Justice Holis doesn't need a martyr. He needs help."

Father Adan sat down on one of the spindly chairs beside his desk. "If there's anything I can do, then I'll do it," he promised. His hands were clenched so tightly his knuckles showed white, but he meant it. Weasel remembered why he liked this priest.

"Nothing dangerous," he said. "I just need information. I know you hear a lot from the priests in other cities."

"We all do," said Father Adan. "It's part of our duty, to notify each other of matters that might affect the church. The One God is the god of man, and all human affairs are in his keeping."

"Yes, I know," said Weasel impatiently. "But does that include . . . illegal affairs?"

Father Adan eyed him cautiously. "It can," he admitted. "What are you fishing for?"

Weasel drew a breath. "I went to the prince," he said. The priest's eyes widened. "I asked him to pardon Justice Holis, but you, you conspirators, were right. He won't stand against Pettibone."

"Hence the conspiracy," said Father Adan. "Weasel, will you

come with me? The last thing Justice Holis would want is to take you down with him."

"If any other justice had caught me," said Weasel, "I'd be in prison right now. Maybe worse. And if the prince can't stand up to Pettibone, I don't think any justice or lawyer is going to do it. We can't save Justice Holis legally, so we have to take him out of the law's hands. It's time for swords, not law books."

"You mean a jailbreak? You're mad! It would take an army!"

"Exactly," said Weasel. "An army that isn't afraid to take on Pettibone—or at least, has nothing to lose by it. An army I know isn't secretly loyal to the regent. I need to find the Falcon."

Arisa made a choking sound, but when Weasel looked at her she was staring at her hands. It had been a pretty outrageous statement, but he needed something outrageous to rescue Justice Holis.

Father Adan frowned. "The Falcon? Weasel, the Falcon's a road bandit. A criminal. A *real* criminal."

"In the country," said Arisa, "they say that the Falcon is a rebel, not a bandit. A rebel against Regent Pettibone, just like you."

"Against the prince, too," said the priest. "If he's not a bandit, why does he steal from carters and common coach passengers? And sometimes kill people who're just trying to defend their possessions?"

Arisa shrugged.

"If he'll fight Pettibone," said Weasel, "if he'll break Justice Holis out of jail, I don't care what else he does."

"Justice Holis would," said Father Adan.

Weasel winced. "Fine. But he has to be alive to lecture me about it. Father Adan, do you know how I can find the Falcon?"

"No," said Father Adan. "If I did know, I'd have to think long and hard about whether or not to tell you. But the only way I know to find the Falcon is to be robbed by him or his men—an experience not everyone survives. The Falcon isn't the only bandit out there either, and some of the others are even more ruthless. It's not a plan I recommend."

Weasel didn't like the idea of being robbed himself. "There has to be another way."

"Weasel . . . " For the first time, the priest hesitated.

"What?"

"I know you're not much of a believer, and ordinarily I wouldn't suggest this to you, but . . . You weren't out on the streets two hours ago, were you? I know you weren't, or you'd have seen them."

"Them? What are you talking about?"

Father Adan's face took on a strange expression, exultant and embarrassed at the same time.

"About two hours ago, three shooting stars crossed the entire sky. Very slowly, all moving in the same direction. It was like . . . It was as if the One God dragged the tips of three fingers across the sky, leaving trails of light behind them."

"So there's a meteor shower," said Weasel. Astronomy was one of Justice Holis' interests, and he had made a point of advancing Weasel's education. Weasel had been wakened to witness several meteor showers, and once he'd been allowed to watch a comet through a telescope. That had been interesting, but educated men now recognized comets and meteors for what they were, instead of taking them for—

"I believe these shooting stars are a portent," Father Adan said firmly. "A message from the One God. I may not be the stuff of martyrs, but I recognize a portent when I see one."

"Father," said Weasel gently, "shooting stars aren't stars. They're big pieces of iron, mixed with some kind of gas that ignites when it touches air. One of the university men traveled all over the world, finding places where they'd crashed and bits of the remains. He wrote a paper about it."

"I know," said Father Adan. "In fact, I've read that paper. But meteors take random paths, they don't follow each other like geese in formation. For three of them to take exactly the same course, at the same moment, lasting the same amount of time . . . Do you know how high the odds against that must be?"

"Astronomical?"

Arisa snickered, and even Father Adan smiled.

"I don't suppose it would do me any good to tell you that I believe the One God is taking a hand in these events, that you should leave saving Holis to him and come away with me?"

Weasel's expression must have answered for him, for the priest sighed.

"Very well. There is one thing I can tell you about the Falcon. It's just a rumor, mind, and it might be dangerous, too, but it's probably less dangerous than setting yourself up to be robbed by armed bandits."

"What is it?"

Father Adan grimaced. "It's *rumored* that the Falcon has connections, dealings some say, with the Hidden."

"The Hidden?" Weasel asked incredulously. "They steal small children and sacrifice them to the old gods, and you think they're *less* dangerous than bandits?"

"That's not true," said Father Adan. "There hasn't been a proven case in several hundred years, and there's even doubt about . . . Well, never mind. But the Hidden are dangerous even if they don't sacrifice children. Their faith has been forbidden by law for over three centuries, so all who practice it are criminals."

"I'm a criminal," said Weasel.

"You *were* a criminal," said Father Adan. "And you know as well as I do that there are criminals, and criminals. You never killed anyone."

Weasel frowned. "I never told you that."

"You didn't have to. The thing is, I'm not sure the Hidden could say the same."

"But you said they didn't sacrifice children."

"They don't. Or I don't think they do. There are some in the church who disagree. But Weasel, you know that many of the country folk are still secretly worshipping the old gods? Sometimes our younger, more passionate priests go into the countryside to convert them. And sometimes, far more often than can be accounted for by simple accident, they don't come back."

Weasel's blood chilled. "You mean they're murdered?"

"I mean that roughly one in fifteen of the priests who go out to bring country people into the church is never heard from again," said Father Adan. "Further than that I don't care to speculate. Though some of my colleagues are less . . . restrained."

Weasel frowned. "But I remember one time, when I was very young, a Hidden leader was *caught* kidnapping a child. I think my mother said he was arrested, but she warned me to be careful of country people if they tried to lure me off."

"Was this about eight years ago?"

Weasel nodded, and Father Adan sighed. "I remember the incident, sadly, for one of our own priests . . . He had been in the countryside, in disguise, trying to identify the Hidden. In order to assist the guard, he claimed, though I'm not sure . . . Anyway, a girl, a toddler, went missing on Sutter Street, by the glassworks there, and this priest saw a man he knew to be a Hidden leader. He revealed the man to the neighborhood, and . . . They were deeply worried about the child, of course, but . . . "

"He was hanged?" Weasel asked. "If the court proved he kidnapped and sacrificed a child, he should have been hanged!"

"He wasn't hanged," said Father Adan grimly. "And he wasn't tried. A mob from the neighborhood tracked him down and stoned him to death. Two days later the little girl was returned, safe and sound. She had climbed into a cart and been carried off to a different part of the city. Since she was too young to tell them who she was, or where her home was, it took the priest there several days to get the word out and find where she belonged."

"So maybe," said Arisa, "the Hidden have good reason to be dangerous."

"Exactly," said Father Adan. "But fortunately, tragedies like that are rare. Contacting the Hidden is probably a lot safer than being robbed at gunpoint."

"Wait a minute," said Weasel. "The Falcon is in contact with the Hidden because they're both criminals, right? So if I could find some other criminals, in the area where the Falcon works, maybe they'd know how to contact him too! Thank you, Father Adan. I think that might work."

"Actually, I don't," said Father Adan. "Even if you did find the Falcon. But if the One God can conjure up so powerful a sign, and draw my eyes to it at just the right moment, perhaps He'll protect you, and Holis, and the others as well. So go with my blessing, whether it means anything to you or not. You're welcome to stay till morning," he added, "but I have bags to pack and papers to burn if I'm going to catch the dawn coach."

Clattering down the stairs after Arisa, Weasel felt more hopeful than he had in some time.

"You're from the country," he said. "Could you put me in touch with the Hidden?"

Arisa snorted. "Not all country folk worship the old gods. Or at least, they don't formally follow the hidden faith. It's more a matter of . . . of customs and rituals. Wait a minute. Who said I was from the country?"

"I guessed," said Weasel. "But you just confirmed it. So could you show me how to contact the Hidden? Or get a message to them, explaining what I need?"

"No," said Arisa bluntly. "The Hidden only reveal themselves to their followers, and I'm told that sometimes they conceal their identity even then. It's not just because they can be arrested, either. Father Adan danced around it, but I've heard that when One God priests come to the countryside, it's not to convert folks. It's to try to learn the identities of the Hidden, so if they go into a city they can be killed. I've also heard that the Hidden being stoned to death by city mobs isn't quite as 'fortunately rare' as Father Adan says it is."

"You think he was lying?" Weasel asked, moving into the kitchen. A shabbily dressed man stood by the kettle, ladling up a bowl of soup.

"Not lying," Arisa admitted. "I don't think that man could lie. But he might not know the truth. He might not want to know."

The man at the kettle turned around. "Weasel, my old chum! I heard you'd got nicked." His smile was wide enough to reveal gaps in his teeth, but the way he set down the newly filled bowl and laid his hand on his belt, next to the hilt of his knife, made Weasel nervous.

"Hello, Gabbo. They nicked Justice Holis, but they weren't interested in small fry like me. I'm looking for a lawyer for him. I'd ask you for a recommendation, but if you knew any good lawyers you wouldn't have spent so much time inside."

"A friend of yours?" Arisa asked.

"Ah, now, Weasel, that's harsh," said Gabbo. He took a long stride, putting himself between them and the church door. "That's a fine shiner you've got. Just like the city guard hands out, if a fellow resists a bit. I wouldn't think Holis had that kind of fist on him."

Gabbo knew he'd been arrested. Gabbo, who'd sell his own mother if the reward was big enough—and his standards of big weren't very high. He would know that if Weasel had escaped, there'd be a big reward.

"I didn't say you were bad," said Weasel, stalling for time. "I said your lawyers were."

He could run back up the stairs, taking Arisa with him. Father Adan would protect him, and if Gabbo threatened Father Adan, half the men who were now asleep in the church would rise against him. But the commotion would bring the guards, Gabbo would tell them that Weasel had come here, and they'd arrest Father Adan. He couldn't go to the priest.

"They did pick me up when they arrested the justice," he told Gabbo. "But they had no charge against me, so they let me go."

For a moment he hoped Gabbo would believe it—it might have been true, after all—but that hope died when Gabbo's hand moved to his knife.

"Weasel, Weasel. You wouldn't lie to your old chum, would you? 'Cause if you are, I've got to ask why, now don't I? Ask myself why, and—"

Arisa darted out of the shadows like a cat. She'd been so quiet Weasel had almost forgotten she was there.

"Wait!" Weasel cried. "He's got a—"

Even though he was facing them, Gabbo barely had time to yank his knife from the sheath before she reached him. As if he needed a knife to deal with a slim young girl, anyway. He grinned and swiped at her; not a serious stroke, just enough to frighten her back into the kitchen.

But Arisa didn't squeal and leap back, as Weasel expected. She ducked, economically, under the blade and then grabbed Gabbo's wrist with her left hand.

Gabbo's eyes widened at the unexpected strength of the grip. Then her right leg swung up in a hard, perfect kick to Gabbo's groin.

Gabbo's eyes grew even wider. Air puffed out of his lungs in a moaning grunt. He doubled over, fell to his knees, and began to retch.

" . . . knife," Weasel finished faintly.

"So he does," said Arisa. She'd kept her hold on Gabbo's arm. Now she bent down and rolled the hilt out of his grasp.

Gabbo, emptying his guts onto the kitchen floor in a stinking flood, hardly seemed aware of what she was doing.

She examined the blade critically, then took a moment to cut off his belt and pull the sheath free.

"Are you coming?" she asked.

Weasel found he'd doubled over himself, in instinctive sympathy, and straightened. "I can't believe you did that!"

He picked his way around Gabbo and followed her into the church.

"He'll recover in a few minutes," said Arisa. "We should get out of here. Fast. Do you know a way to get out of the city without being seen? I suspect he won't follow us into the countryside; he looks like the city sewer type."

"Several ways out. I can't believe you did that."

Arisa opened the big church door. Fresh night air bathed Weasel's face.

"Why not?" she asked. "He was going to turn you over to the guard. If he's a sample, I don't think much of your friends. Besides, I wanted a knife, and now I've got one."

Weasel grabbed her arm, dragging her to a stop. "Who are you?"

"Arisa Benison. Just like I told you." Her eyes met his calmly in the dim lamplight. "Do you really want to stand here all night? If he catches us, he's likely to be testy. As your bodyguard, I don't recommend it."

"Bodyguard?"

"Well, you need some kind of keeper. And you did help me break out of that cell. So we'll start off toward my home, and I'll try to help you contact the Hidden along the way. Though I can't promise that," she finished soberly. "They really do hide themselves. They have reason."

Weasel eyed the knife. Arisa sheathed it and then stuck it through her belt. She handled it as casually, as expertly, as Gabbo himself. Maybe more so.

"I'm not worried," said Weasel. "If we can defeat both Gabbo and the palace dungeons, the Hidden don't stand a chance."

CHAPTER 5

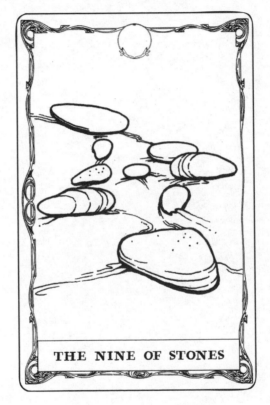

THE NINE OF STONES

The Nine of Stones: withe.
To be one with nature, spiritual harmony, magic.

5

"I hate nature," Weasel grumbled, scraping mud off his shoe with a stick.

"Give it a chance," Arisa told him. "You only made nature's acquaintance a few hours ago."

"I've been in the country before." Weasel had, though he could count those excursions on the fingers of one hand. "Most of it's dirty, and the bits that are clean are either boring, or they smell like horses."

"Horses smell good," said Arisa. "Better than people, by far. And look at the leaves. Look at the sunshine. This is glorious!" She flung out her arms as if to embrace the scene around them.

It didn't look glorious to Weasel. The track beside the road, where they were walking, wasn't quite as muddy as the road was, or the bare fields where crops had been taken up and cows grazed on the stubble. And added their droppings to the muck. She'd made no claim, he noted, that cows smelled better. He had to admit that the few remaining leaves were an artistic blend of gold and deep red, but there weren't many left. And he was suspicious of air this fresh. It felt like some busy housewife had swept his lungs clean, and when he next breathed real air he'd start coughing.

"At least you're not too badly dressed for it," Arisa added. "I'm sorry about your shoes."

"That's all right," said Weasel, though his shoes would never be the same. It would have been ungracious to complain—the only reason he wasn't splattering mud on a footman's pale britches was because they'd stopped before leaving the city to extract Arisa's bag from the inn where she'd been staying. They hadn't wanted to show themselves, so Weasel's lock picks had come into play, opening the cupboard where the innkeeper stored abandoned belongings. At least he hadn't yet sold them.

Arisa's britches were a bit wide in the hip, and long at the knee, but the rest of her boy's clothes fit Weasel well enough. It wasn't that he was small, Weasel assured himself. She was big. A fine, strapping, country wench.

He eyed the slim figure walking ahead of him, carrying the battered leather satchel since his turn to carry it had just ended. She wasn't a strapping wench. He might have taken her for a particularly slight boy, except for the thick braid tumbling down her back.

When they'd stopped in a shadowed alley, so Weasel could change his filthy palace footman's clothing for something less conspicuous, there had been a skirt in her bag.

When he'd asked why she didn't wear the skirt, she'd laughed at him. Looking at the mud that splattered his stockings, and the droplets of dew still clinging to the high, brown grass that pressed on both sides of the path, Weasel now understood her desire to wear britches. He only wished she'd carried a second pair of boots. They might have pinched, for her feet, at least, were smaller than his, but at this point he'd have traded pinching for dryness.

"Cheer up," said Arisa. "We're nearly to Brimming Creek.

We'll get an early luncheon there, and maybe you can make one of the stable boys a trade."

"Good city shoes for clod-crushing country boots?" Weasel asked. "He'd have to be out of his mind."

Brimming Creek was a typical country village, just like many others Weasel had ridden through in Justice Holis' coach on the rare occasions when he had business in the country that required a clerk. It had the same stone streets, and the same thatched roofs. It held the same simply clad people; the men with their loose, shoulder-length hair and shapeless, broad-brimmed hats, the women with their kerchiefs, and braids down their backs.

But now, walking among them, Weasel noticed that most of their faces were not only browner than city folks of the same class, but rounder. Even those with patched, worn clothing had a well-fed look you just didn't see among the city's poor.

But an even bigger difference was the way they met his eyes, and smiled or nodded as he passed. It was nothing familiar or obtrusive, just an acknowledgment of his presence, sometimes accompanied by a cheery "Good day t' you."

If you acknowledged everyone you met walking down a city street, you'd spend your whole life nodding and "good-day"-ing. Still, he didn't feel as awkward as he'd expected when Arisa led him into the local inn. No great coaching inn this, with dozens of rooms to let and more city accents in the public tap room than country ones. The Suckling Boar, too close to the city for coaches to stop, was more tavern than inn.

The taproom was cleaner than most city taverns, and it held only a handful of customers. It was too early for luncheon, though the scent of roasting goose made Weasel's mouth water.

Arisa walked up to a big-armed man in an apron, who was wiping down tables. "We're on the road, Goodman, and looking for a meal."

Weasel's eyes widened; her accent would fit right into this village. Not as broad as some he'd heard, but definitely country.

"We've not much coin," she added. "But we're willing to work."

The tapster, who might have been the innkeeper himself for all Weasel knew, eyed their muddy feet sympathetically. "Shank's mare? You may be sorry for it in a few days. They say the rain's coming back on us."

"Not just yet, I hope," said Arisa.

"Couple of days." His gaze came to rest on Weasel's shoes and he frowned, then shrugged. "Can you muck out a stall?"

"Of course," said Arisa, not bothering to consult Weasel about the matter.

As it happened, he was familiar with the task. He'd done a lot of odd jobs before he perfected his craft as pickpocket. Still . . .

"The reason I took up my . . . previous profession was because I don't like mucking stalls," Weasel told her, forking a dark mass of straw, and other matter, into a wheelbarrow. "And we don't have time for this! Less than two weeks . . . We have to travel faster, not waste so much time working for room and meals!"

Arisa snorted. "There's no point in traveling faster when you don't know where you're going. And it's hard to make speed if you're fainting from hunger. We don't have enough money between us to buy more than two meals. Did you smell that goose?"

"Yes, but there are other ways," said Weasel. "I could manage."

Arisa snorted. "And the moment someone missed their purse, they'd go straight after one of the dozens of pickpockets who doubtless haunt this village, completely ignoring the only two strangers in the room?"

Weasel blushed. She was right. He was probably the only pickpocket this village had ever seen, so if any crime was committed . . .

"We'd better hope no one decides that today is a good day for a murder," he said. "Given that a stranger would get the blame."

"Not for murder," said Arisa. "People only murder people they know well enough to hate. No one kills a stranger. Well, not often. Not in the country."

The goose was stuffed with apples and onions, and served with cooked greens and fresh rolls, with a bit of bread pudding for the sweet. No wonder these people looked so well fed!

Weasel even managed to trade the stable boy, who came to inspect the job they'd done, for a pair of boots he claimed were his second best. Weasel was pretty sure he was about to discard them, for the heels were worn down on the side, and the soles were thin enough that Weasel could feel the cobblestones beneath his feet. But that was only fair, because he told the stable boy the mud would come right off his shoes, and when they dried they'd be good as new.

"He still got a better deal," Weasel told Arisa as he trudged, more happily now, down the muddy path.

"Just another bumpkin," she sighed, "taken in by a fast-talking townsman. You think he doesn't know what those shoes are worth?"

Weasel grinned. "So when do we start looking for the Hidden?"

"When we're closer to the Falcon's territory," said Arisa. "He doesn't rob people right next to the city. Maybe because the guard's too close."

"You know where the Falcon works?"

Arisa snorted. "Everyone who travels knows where the Falcon works, and other bandits, too. I'm my mother's business representative, remember? Sometimes I carry money for her."

"Is that why you learned to use a knife?" Weasel asked. She'd attached the sheath to her own belt and slid it behind her hip so the skirts of her coat concealed it, but Weasel hadn't forgotten it was there. "I'd think a pistol would be easier for you, and more deadly."

"Yes, but Gabbo didn't have a pistol."

Weasel stopped, staring. "Are you saying that if Gabbo'd had a pistol, you'd have taken that away from him? Just like you took the knife?"

"Of course not," said Arisa.

Weasel felt his shoulders sag with relief. At least she wasn't crazy enough to—

"When you take a pistol from someone you have to push their hand *up*. So if they fire, the ball goes into the ceiling. And you have to be closer when you start your move too. And besides..."

The quiver in her voice gave her away.

"You're putting me on!" Weasel exclaimed, and she broke down and laughed aloud.

"You should have seen your face."

She was joking. He was almost sure of it. He was about to pursue the matter further when something caught his gaze.

"Why is there a doll nailed to that fence?" he asked. "I've been seeing them all day."

"It's not a doll," said Arisa. "Remember when I told you that in the country, worship of the old gods was more a matter of customs than of real faith? This is the kind of thing I mean. The farmer who owns this field may never have prayed to any god in his life, but he still puts up a straw lady to bring the Lady's blessing to his crop."

"The Lady. Is she one of the old gods? Or goddesses?" Weasel knew very little about the old gods, he suddenly realized, beyond the teaching of the One God's priests that they were all false gods, and the followers of the One God should avoid such heathen abominations.

"She's the only god anyone in the country mentions much," said Arisa. "And again, it's more a matter of putting up a straw lady, or saying things like 'Lady bless us!' when a goodwife hears some scandalous gossip."

"So it's more like . . . like a superstition than a real faith. Like thinking anyone with the sword and shield that were lost is the true king of Deorthas."

Arisa snorted. "It's not that whoever has them is the true king. Unless they've been destroyed, someone else has them right now. What the old folks say is that the true king's *power* comes from the sword and the shield. That since they were lost, the kings aren't half the kings they were 'in the old days.' But since kings have been ruling without them for centuries, that's clearly just another foolish country superstition. One so silly that your Regent Pettibone has offered a thousand gold blessings to get them back."

Weasel grinned. "Your point. But he's not my regent. And the reason he wants the sword and shield, according to Justice Holis, is because it would make the country folk happier with his rule. Just like he's tried to please the townsmen by enforcing the end-of-shift bell."

"Does he really enforce that?" Arisa asked curiously. "I've heard that lots of mill workers are kept at their jobs long past the end of the workday, till they're almost dropping from exhaustion. And that if they complain, their employers fire them and find someone poor and desperate enough to take their place. But I wondered. . . . Parents mostly tell that kind of story when their children start talking about going to the city to get better jobs."

"It's sort of true and sort of not," Weasel told her. "Some owners stop the work shift right on the bell, unless they have an urgent job. And those owners, the good ones, will pay a bit extra if they keep their people over. The bad ones . . . "

He looked at the rain-washed fields, empty except for twittering birds that fluttered from bush to bush. He could understand why someone would get bored with it, but still . . .

"I wouldn't advise people to go to the city for a job. Not unless they're already skilled in some trade, and even then they could get into a bad situation pretty easily."

"So if the regent's enforcing the end of shift, he's doing something good," said Arisa thoughtfully.

"Yes," Weasel admitted. It was one of the few things the regent had done that Justice Holis approved of. "Pettibone's city-bred. Justice Holis says that Pettibone believes that he took over the regency so he could fix the city's problems."

Arisa grinned. "But you don't believe it?"

"If someone gains a lot of wealth or power by doing something, I don't look very hard for another motive. But Justice Holis says people are more complex than that, and he's usually right. On the other hand, Pettibone started his regency by hanging half the navy, so it's hard to believe that mercy was his main motivation."

"Even in the country we know about that," said Arisa. "He hanged only officers, but many of the common sailors are countrymen, and they talk about it."

"He didn't really hang half the navy," Weasel admitted. "Just the officers who supported Admiral Hastings' bid for the regency."

"But that was more than half the officers," said Arisa. "And the king had chosen Admiral Hastings as regent. It was his right, his duty, to—"

"He claimed that the king had chosen him," Weasel interrupted. "No documents confirming that were ever found."

"Of course not. Pettibone was the chief justice, and he had control of the palace for more than a week after the king's death. He'd been feuding with the admiral for years, because the admiral was trying to persuade the king to stop favoring the city over the country! Pettibone would have destroyed anything that supported the admiral. And if he had the right, why hang not only the admiral, but all the officers who were loyal to him? If the lord commander of the army hadn't backed Pettibone against the navy, he wouldn't be regent today!"

Justice Holis had considered the loyalty of the army key to the conspiracy's success, but Weasel wasn't about to discuss that with someone who was almost a stranger—and a curiously well-informed stranger, at that.

"You know a lot about this for a country girl."

Arisa shrugged. "Country folk don't like Regent Pettibone. Which you should understand, since you tried to overthrow him yourself."

"Not me!" Weasel exclaimed. "I only copied letters for Justice Holis. I don't care who rules anything, as long as I can keep out of their way."

Arisa came to a stop, right in front of a large puddle, staring at him. "You don't mean that. You were *involved* in the conspiracy."

"Justice Holis was involved," said Weasel. "And look where it got him."

"But . . . but if you see injustice, if you see that things are wrong, you have to care! You have to try to fix them."

"No, you don't," said Weasel, picking his way through the mud-filled ruts. "It's stupid to care."

Arisa followed him. "So you think I'm stupid to help you find the Hidden?"

"Ah . . ."

"Why would I do that, if I didn't care about injustice? And want to stop it?"

"We haven't even tried to find them yet," Weasel complained.

"We've just reached the outskirts of the Falcon's territory," Arisa told him. "I'll ask at the village where we stop this evening. I'm not afraid to do what's right!"

Washing a mountain of dirty dishes bought Weasel and Arisa dinner, breakfast, and a pallet on the floor in the inn's laundry room. The floor was stone, and noise from the kitchen, which lay on the other side of the open hearth, carried through—but as Arisa pointed out, at least it was warm.

They were wakened in the morning by the innkeeper's wife, when she let the laundresses in. She wore a lace-trimmed cap instead of the more usual kerchief, and her manner was brisk, but not unkind.

Weasel was stumbling off to wash when Arisa grabbed his

arm. "Goodwife, may we ask you something? It's a bit private."

Surprise deepened the lines on the woman's forehead. "You can ask anything, though I make no promise to answer."

She gestured for Arisa and Weasel to follow her into the corridor, which was empty at this early hour. She folded her arms and waited.

"My friend here is trying to find the Hidden," Arisa said bluntly. "Nothing harmful to them or him. He needs some information they might have."

The woman's eyes widened. "I can't help you there, m'girl. I don't know anyone who follows the old faith. Or if I do, I don't know it."

"Oh, I figured that," said Arisa swiftly. "It just seemed to me that you'd meet a lot of people. In an inn, and all. You might be in a position to spread word that he's looking."

"I might at that," said the woman. "But I don't know if I should. Bluntly, m'boy, I'd advise you to find some other source of information. The Hidden don't want to be found."

"I understand," said Weasel, fighting down a surge of disappointment. "If I could pay—"

"It's important," Arisa interrupted. "Important to him, and might be desperately important to other good folks. He's city-bred," she added apologetically, though Weasel had no idea what she was apologizing for.

"Humph." The woman looked back and forth between them. "Well, this has been an odd conversation. It's probably worth gossiping about. What direction are you going from here?"

"West," said Arisa. "All the way to Thimbleton, in time. Thank you, goodwife. Thank you very much."

"Why did you thank her?" Weasel asked, as they trudged along the footpath beside the road. It was drier today, the One God be praised. "She didn't offer to contact the Hidden. She didn't offer to do anything except gossip."

Arisa rolled her eyes in disgust. "And you thought you didn't need a guide."

"You said you were my bodyguard."

"Whatever. But gossip *spreads* in the countryside. If there are any Hidden within twenty miles of that village, within a few days they'll know you're looking for them. What they do about it is up to them."

"I don't want to do them any harm," Weasel told her. "I want to ask a favor!"

"Yes, but they can't be sure of that. You could be a One God fanatic, plotting to assassinate them all."

"Then they could turn me in to the guard," said Weasel, skirting a puddle. "The law says that violence will not be tolerated in any god's name. That's why the Hidden faith was forbidden in the first place, because of the sacrifices. Any One God follower who commits violence against the Hidden is breaking the law and can be punished."

"That may be the law on the books," said Arisa. "But it will only be law in reality if someone enforces it."

"No one can enforce it if the Hidden don't complain," Weasel pointed out.

"But in order to complain they have to admit to being followers of the Hidden faith, and then they get arrested for that.
Which reminds me, what were you doing trying to pay that
woman?"

"I wasn't trying to pay her. We don't have anything to pay her
with. I was apologizing for not being able to make it worth her
while. Why should she do favors for me?"

"Because you need help," said Arisa. "Because it's important.
Isn't your God's main teaching that people should care about
each other?"

"'Man must look after man,'" Weasel quoted. "That's why he's
not my god. I care about me first, me second, and nobody else.
That's how you survive. Caring about people gets you into as
much trouble as caring about causes."

"Really? Then why are you tramping down the road, with no
money, looking for people who might kill you, if you don't *care*
about your justice?"

Weasel scowled. "That's different. Justice Holis is . . . is . . . "

Arisa waited.

" . . . different."

Arisa laughed. "Why? You care about him."

"And look at the trouble it's gotten me into," Weasel told her
gloomily. "I might not even survive it."

That afternoon they swept out a bakeshop in exchange for several
loaves of day-old bread, and the baker's grandmother agreed to gossip with her customers about a young city boy who was looking for

the Hidden as he traveled the road to the west.

They reached Huckstable that evening and while they waited tables in the common room, to earn their supper and bed, Arisa found a couple of old men who weren't averse to spreading a bit of gossip.

For luncheon the next afternoon they mucked out a cattle pen, finding no one to spread their message except the cows. And before they could reach the next town, the rain came on.

The morning had started out clear, but by noon a brisk breeze was pushing heavy clouds across the sky, and by midafternoon the thunderheads had grouped together like a gang of street toughs, rumbling to warn the ordinary citizens of their intent.

Arisa spotted the hay shed just as the first thick drops began to fall. They raced over the stubbled fields and reached its shelter moments before the skies opened and the torrent poured down.

"Too bad it's so cold," Weasel said, half-shouting to make himself heard over the pounding of rain on the roof. "We could almost bathe in this."

"At least we're dry."

"Until the roof starts to leak."

Arisa gave him a disgusted look. "It's a hay shed, city boy. If the roof leaks, the hay gets moldy. Hay sheds have the best roofs in the countryside."

Weasel was skeptical, but the roof proved amazingly tight, and nestling into the hay offered them a bit of warmth as they watched the hard rain settle into a steady drizzle.

"It'll be over in a few hours," Arisa predicted. "We can make it to the next inn, though it may be dark by the time we get there."

"But until then we're stuck here," said Weasel. Only eleven days till Justice Holis' trial began. Of course trials could last for weeks, or months . . . or days, if Regent Pettibone wanted them to end quickly.

"Unless you want to walk in the rain, catch pneumonia, and—"

"I'm not stupid," said Weasel. "It's just . . . Never mind. I wish we had a deck of cards or some dice. At least we'd have something to do."

Arisa laughed. "Hasn't anybody told you to be careful what you wish for?" She lifted the battered satchel onto her lap and dug into it, finally pulling out a deck of arcana cards. "Wish and it shall be granted!"

"I wish for a hot pork pie."

"One miracle at a time."

"I'll take it," said Weasel happily. He swept hay off a section of the floor. "Four-card runs, chaos is out, not wild, and two hundred points ends a round. Or do you prefer three-card runs?"

Arisa was already shuffling, with a deftness that should have warned him. "Three-card runs are for babes and amateurs. What are we playing for?"

"What have we got?" Weasel asked.

Over the next several hours, Weasel's vast fortune of hay gradually became Arisa's even vaster fortune of hay.

"We'd better stop," she said finally. "I win the rest of the stack, and you won't have anything left to tuck into. You'd freeze. Besides, it's beginning to let up."

Weasel looked out at the rain. It was lessening, but it still fell steadily. He had no desire to be drenched. "Not quite yet. Who taught you to play arcanara? Will he teach me?"

"He's a friend of my mother's," Arisa told him. "And I don't know if he'd teach you or not. He might, if you happen to meet him."

"Oh. One of *those* friends?"

"You can say smuggler here. There's no one around to eavesdrop except the mice, and they don't talk to the law."

Weasel shuffled the cards idly, liking the feel of the deck. He cut it and looked down at the pictured woman. Wind swirled her archaic gown and flung her black hair out like a banner. She walked upon storm clouds, and lightning shot from the places where she stepped.

"The storm. How appropriate."

"Not really. The storm doesn't mean a simple storm, it signifies anything that brings good and bad in the same package. Floods, but also water for crops. A lot of the water cards are like that."

"It signifies? You're not one of those . . . I mean, you don't believe you can tell fortunes with these things, do you?"

Arisa's chin rose defiantly. "Yes. Haven't you ever had your fortune told with cards?"

"I've seen people do it. Make a fair amount of money at it too. But it's only . . . "

" . . . a foolish country superstition? It isn't. These cards, the images, they used to be the old gods. A lot of them, at least. That's why the storm isn't shown as just a storm, it's the goddess of storms. The man who taught me to tell fortunes—this is a different man, not the one who taught me to play arcanara—he said almost all the cards with a person on them used to be gods, and even some that don't show people. Here." She took the deck and sorted through it. "The lady of stones. She's the Lady. The one the country folk care about. She's the goddess of earth and harvest. If she comes up in your fortune, she signifies wealth, fertility, and peace."

"Could I skip the fertility part?" Weasel asked. "Who wants a pile of brats to feed?"

Arisa shrugged. "I think you'd find peace pretty boring too."

"You're wrong about that." Weasel watched the cards flow through her hands. "I've had too much excitement in my life. I *like* peace."

Arisa looked skeptical.

"I do! But I've seen con men telling fortunes. It's pretty obvious that they just interpret the cards into whatever their mark wants to hear."

"That's true," Arisa admitted. "For people who don't have any withe. But if you have got withe, my friend said it surfaces when you tell the cards. He said I had quite a lot of it."

"With? With what?"

"Withe," said Arisa patiently. "It sounds the same, but it's a thing in itself. It means being one with the earth; with Deorthas' earth magic. Just a minute."

She went through the deck again and pulled out the nine of stones. It showed nine stones, lying in the sandy curve of a streambed.

Weasel frowned. "They make up a star, don't they?"

"You've got a good eye," Arisa told him. "The star ties this card to the stars suit, as well as stones, since one of its aspects is spiritual harmony, and spiritual things are the province of stars. But most people don't even see it. Harr— my friend would have said you probably have some withe yourself."

Weasel snorted. "I have as much earth magic as those stones do. Less. It sounds like your friend would be a good person to ask about the Hidden, if he knows so much about the old gods and all."

"He might have been." Arisa's voice was calm, but she kept her eyes on the cards. "He's dead. Do you want to know your fortune?"

Weasel didn't, but he recognized an attempt to change the subject when he heard it. "Sure. Why not?"

Arisa shuffled the deck again. "The first card in the spread is your significator," she told him, sounding just like every con man he'd ever heard. "It represents you, your essence—or sometimes a powerful force that's affecting your life."

Or whatever the fortune-teller says it represents. But Weasel kept the sardonic thought to himself, and Arisa drew the top card and laid it on the floor.

The card showed a man hanging upside down from a rope tied to one ankle. He looked remarkably composed for someone whose throat had just been cut.

A chill pricked Weasel's spine. He'd had nightmares about hanging all the years he'd been picking pockets. He still had them sometimes. "How cheery."

Arisa sighed. "Be as skeptical as you want. It won't affect the truth of the cards."

The con men said that, too.

"So I'm going to get my throat cut? Not if I have anything to say about it."

"No," said Arisa. "The hanged man represents a voluntary sacrifice, for the greater good. It might mean as much as . . . as a soldier laying down his life in battle, or as little as denying yourself some trifle and giving the money to the poor."

"Voluntary sacrifice for the greater good. That represents me. Absolutely."

"This is your significator, so right now it does," Arisa told him. "Whether you know it or not."

Weasel stared at her. "You really do believe in this, don't you?"

"Yes," said Arisa simply. "I've seen it come true too many times. At least, when I lay the cards. The card that goes beneath the significator is what supports you. It represents a power, or principle, or person, that you can rely on."

The rock was a stones card, of course. It showed not only a rock, but also a knight in old-fashioned armor.

"Was he a god too?" Weasel asked, keeping his voice casual.

"He probably was, once. Now he represents courage, strength, and perseverance. All qualities that come from within, by the way. So you must not be the weak-willed city brat I took you for."

"Thank you *so* much," Weasel told her, but he was grateful for the lighter mood.

Arisa grinned at him. "The card that goes above you is what inspires or guides you." She turned over the four of stars, showing a book-filled library.

"The book," said Weasel. "Another card that's completely inappropriate for me."

"It's actually knowledge," Arisa told him. "Books, learning, science. All the good things that come from the exercise of the intellect. It can also represent a person who has those qualities."

As Justice Holis did?

"Go on," said Weasel. He hoped she couldn't tell that this was getting to him.

"To your left is what misleads you," Arisa continued. "This is something that might fool you, or lure you away from your proper path."

She laid down the five of waters. "Mistrust. Being a waters card, it can also mean trusting something you shouldn't, but in this case, I think it means that you should be more trusting."

Weasel snickered. "Not much chance of that."

"Proving that the cards are right," Arisa countered. "But between you and what misleads you lies what counsels you. What offers you true guidance."

The six of waters showed a cloaked figure, with a staff in hand and a pack on its back, walking toward a village. It was evening in the card; lamplight glowed in the windows, but the doors were closed.

"The stranger," Arisa told him. "Someone or something new arriving in your life. That's probably me," she added. "So remember to be trusting when I ask you for all your money."

Weasel laughed aloud. "You've already got all the hay. Don't be greedy."

"To your far right, what threatens you," said Arisa, drawing the next card. "This is something that might thwart you, or . . . "

"What?" Weasel asked. The moonless night was a fires card, which had always seemed strange to him. "So the cards say it's going to get dark soon. They're right."

"Moonless night doesn't mean darkness," said Arisa. "Not physical darkness. It signifies someone with malicious intent. Without conscience or pity."

"Pettibone to the life," said Weasel flippantly.

"It's not funny," Arisa told him. "Have you noticed how many major arcana cards are in this layout? This is a powerful fortune, about powerful forces. As for Pettibone . . . There are rumors, in the countryside, that he murdered the old king. If this is him," she gestured to the dark card on the hanged man's right, "then it might be true."

"We have that rumor in the city, too," Weasel told her. "But Justice Holis says the king died in a hunting accident, when his horse took a jump badly. It wasn't like his saddle fell off either. Nothing was tampered with. The horse slipped in some mud, fell on the king, and crushed him."

The justice and his cohorts had looked into that accident thoroughly. Weasel had copied several letters about it.

"Well, this is what, or who, defends you," said Arisa. She laid a final card between the hanged man and the moonless night, and frowned.

"The two of waters?" Weasel asked. "A lousy two is all I get?"

"It's a discovery," Arisa told him. "A discovery, or sometimes recovering something that was lost. But how that could defend you from . . . Anyway, that's it." She swept up the cards, smiling at Weasel with a false brightness that made him far more nervous than her previous scowl. "The rain's about over. Shall we go?"

Setting a brisk pace, they managed to reach the small village of Sweetsprings just after dark. The tavern keeper—they didn't even bother to call the place an inn—allowed them to dry their soaked boots in front of the hearth fire, while they wiped down the tables and swept the common-room floor. The tavern closed shortly after they reached the village, for the rain had kept people away. But the lack of customers meant there was plenty of food available, and the tavern keeper gave them space in front of the kitchen fire, a couple of straw pallets, and blankets, too.

A heavy meal, and the hot tea the tavern keeper had provided to warm his workers, produced the logical result: Weasel woke up in the middle of the night with an urgent need to visit the privy. At least his boots were dry.

Cursing under his breath, Weasel carried his boots away from the hearth so he wouldn't wake Arisa when he put them on. By the time he reached the kitchen door, at the far side of the room from the fireplace, he was shivering. By the time he'd finished in the privy and stepped out into the damp night, his teeth were chattering. But even if they hadn't been, he might not have heard the soft sounds that could have warned him.

His first intimation of trouble was a blanket falling over his head. He started to move, to shout, but two arms went round him. One imprisoned his arms, lifting him clear off his feet. The other clamped over his mouth, pinning his head against a hard shoulder.

He couldn't shout and he couldn't run. Weasel braced himself to kick.

"Don't do it, m'boy." A man's deep voice, with a note in it that made Weasel hesitate before he even finished the threat. "You'll be sorrier for it than I, I promise you. Besides"—the hard chest pressed against Weasel's back shook with sudden laughter—"I'm told you *want* to find the Hidden. More fool you, if it's true. Is it?"

Weasel froze. The Hidden? Here? Now?

"*Is it?*" The powerful grip tightened warningly.

Weasel nodded, as much as he could.

"Then I don't have to worry about you kicking, do I? For you've found us."

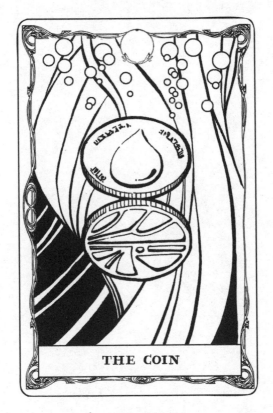

CHAPTER 6

THE COIN

The Coin: opposites in one.
Things are not always what they seem.

There were two of them, Weasel discovered. While the strong one held him, the other strapped his arms to his body using something that, through the thick blanket, felt like a couple of belts.

Weasel made no move to resist. He didn't even try to shout when the strong man got careless and let the hand over his mouth slip. Perhaps because of that they let him walk out of the inn yard, steering him with a hand on his shoulder.

It seemed to be quite a long walk, which was difficult when you couldn't see, but Weasel didn't ask them to remove the blanket. He was passionately grateful for that blanket, for if they took it off, if they allowed him to see their faces, he would probably die. Father Adan was wrong about the Hidden being safer. Men who took precautions like this to protect their identity would kill as surely as any bandit would. So Weasel stumbled on without complaint, over fields and ditches and across several roads, before the hand on his shoulder drew him to a halt.

"Take the blanket off him," said a man's voice calmly. "I want to see his face."

"No!" The straps pinning his arms fell away. "I mean, I don't—"

He clutched the blanket with numb hands, holding it against the tugs that tried to pull it loose.

"Stop," said the man's voice. The tension on the blanket

ceased abruptly. "You can bury yourself in it if you like, m'boy, but it's safe to look. We're all masked."

Someone gasped. "He thought we'd ... we'd ... That's ridiculous! Of all the—"

"It's not ridiculous," said the calm voice. "It's a very logical conclusion."

"I thought he wasn't supposed t' be logical," a woman said.

A woman? And why shouldn't he be logical? Weasel pulled the blanket away from his face. They were masked, with kerchiefs tied over their noses and chins and also across their foreheads, leaving only a slit for their eyes. They wore hooded cloaks, pulled tight around them, to disguise their bodies as well. He would never be able to identify these people—and they probably wouldn't have gone to so much trouble to ensure that if they intended to kill him.

It gave Weasel enough courage that when one of them tried to take the blanket he pulled back, and then wrapped it around himself.

"I need this. You've all got coats under those cloaks." Without a kerchief to cover his face, the words emerged in a puff of steam.

"So we do," said the calm voice. "Logical again."

Weasel looked around. There were five of them, shapeless shadows in the moonlight, standing in a small clearing between the edge of a forest and a weathered building that had probably been a barn. Abandoned, for there were holes in the wall, and no smell of animals in the cold air.

"Why shouldn't I be logical?" Weasel asked.

"I think you should," said the calm-voiced man. He seated

himself on the bottom rail of an old fence; the top rail was gone. "Logical is part of the job, in my opinion."

"The sign of the heart, of the heart's wisdom, adjoins his constellation," said the woman firmly. "Wisdom isn't a matter of logic."

"Spoken with the illogic of someone who thinks that the hammer is the sign of the heart," the deep voice of Weasel's captor retorted.

He turned to study the strong man and fought down a shiver. This was someone he might be able to identify, for he stood half a head taller than any of the rest, bulky as an ox. But he sounded like a scholar, in one of the university debates that Justice Holis had dragged Weasel to attend, as he went on hotly, "The hammer is clearly the symbol of the Sky Lord's victory over Abriar. Or perhaps Boraldis. But either way—"

"It only looks like a hammer if you want it to look like a hammer," the woman snapped. "Its placement clearly indicates—"

"They go on like this all the time," the calm voice said. "Ignore them. You should be logical, as well as wise, if you're the one we're looking for."

"Looking for?" Weasel's head spun. The only name he'd recognized from that farrago was Abriar, and Abriar was a month, not a person. "I'm the one who's looking for you." Why had he ever thought that was a good idea?

"Yes, that was convenient." Was Calm Voice the leader? The others had fallen silent when he spoke.

"Why are you looking for me?"

"We're not," said another of them. He sounded almost prim, his country accent not as broad as the strong man's had been. "And I, for one, am certain of it. A common thief can't be the one we seek."

"How did you know I was a thief?" Weasel demanded. Outrage was swiftly turning to alarm.

"He was a thief," said Calm Voice. "Now he's a clerk. Who knows what he may become."

"Not that." The prim man sniffed. "He might even be faking it, if he knows the secret."

"How could he know the secret? It was lost even before the symbols disappeared. But there's a simple way to find out," said Calm Voice. "What were you doing three nights ago, boy?"

"Three nights?" So much had happened that he had to think about it. "I was breaking out of the palace dungeon. Well, not really the dungeon, though it was a cell. But if you know I'm a clerk . . . " How did they know so much? " . . . then you must know whose. You know that Justice Holis and the others have been arrested."

"I heard about it." Calm Voice didn't sound very interested, but Weasel sensed that was a lie. "It was a nice conspiracy, even if he did bring in the wrong church. But it's doomed now—unless this really is the time. Breaking out of a cell is all you did? Do you know what you were doing at the moment the shooting stars crossed the sky?"

"The shoot—You don't think that's a portent of something, do you? Meteors and comets are only . . . "

They all stared, as if they were measuring Weasel for something, paying no attention to his words. What had he meant about Holis bringing in the wrong church? Who cared if they believed the stars were a portent?

"I was breaking out of a cell," said Weasel. "I didn't even see them."

The prim one snorted. "There. I told you."

"That's not conclusive." It was another woman, with a deeper voice than the first. "Not conclusive either way."

Weasel wished they'd either explain what they were talking about or stop talking about it.

"I need some information from you," he said. "You know that Justice Holis and his friends were arrested for conspiring against the regent. The regent will hang them if they come to trial, so I have to get them out of prison before that. Break them out. Which means I need armed men. Lots of them."

"You need more than armed men to assault the palace," said Calm Voice. He sounded amused. "You'd need a real army, with cannons, for that. And we aren't even armed men."

"I know," said Weasel. "But I think I can get a bunch of armed men into the palace, through the same route I got out. So I don't need a whole army, just enough to take the palace guard by surprise. A hundred or so."

They watched him in thoughtful silence.

"Maybe he is," said the strong man.

The prim man snorted. "If you think that harebrained scheme indicates anything but an overactive imagination, you're as foolish as he is."

"Not foolish," said Calm Voice gently. "Desperate. But we don't have any armed men, much less a hundred. Why seek us out?"

"Because"—Weasel drew a deep breath—"someone said you could help me contact the Falcon."

"The Falcon?" There was honest astonishment in the calm voice. "The road bandit? Why would we know anything about him?"

"Well, someone said . . . And you're both operating outside the law. So I thought . . . "

The strong man snorted. "City-bred. We've no more dealings with the Falcon, or any other bandit, than any honest man. We *wouldn't* deal with him. I've seen the bodies of folk he's shot, carried into my village."

"Maybe," said Weasel. "But I need armed men, a lot of them, soon. The Falcon has them. Will you help me?"

"Why should we?" the first woman asked. "Criminals that we are."

"I've been thinking about that," said Weasel eagerly. "According to my friend, you haven't sacrificed anyone in several centuries, which means none of you ever did. And if you'd agree to go on not sacrificing people, there's no reason for your faith to be outlawed. If you helped free a bunch of justices . . . If Pettibone is banished . . . You could bring a suit, and maybe get the law that proscribes your faith rescinded."

The calm-voiced man threw back his head and laughed. "Bring suit! You *are* the one, whatever the others think. Oh, don't be offended, I'm not laughing at you. It's a good idea, in its way, but I'm afraid it's not practical. As long as the townsmen hate us, and the regent—or whoever's in power—needs peace in the city, we're going to remain outside the law."

"But if you help me, you'll have a chance to overthrow Pettibone and earn the new regent's gratitude! He could make your faith legal!"

The calm-voiced man stood and laid his hands on Weasel's shoulders. "I hope you succeed in your quest, m'boy. I pray to every god in the pantheon—and I know them all—that you'll pass your test. That you become what you must, if we're to have any hope of coming into the light. But I tell you in truth, I have no more idea of how to find the Falcon than you do. Maybe less, for I've never thought about it."

Weasel knew truth when he heard it. "Then why did you bring me here?" he cried. "What's this about, if you can't help me?"

"We'd help you if we could," the man said. "For you are the first step. But we have no way to break your friend out of jail. I don't know how to contact the Falcon—at least, not without getting shot in the process. And this is your test, not mine." He turned to the strong man. "Take him back to the tavern."

"Wait! You can't just . . ."

They turned away, vanishing swiftly into the woods that surrounded the clearing. Within moments, only the strong man remained. Though it wasn't as if he needed any help to keep Weasel from following them, or doing anything else that he didn't want Weasel to do.

"Put the blanket over your head," he said, pulling a long strap from beneath his cloak.

Weasel thought about arguing. Walking blind wasn't easy, and he hadn't seen any of them. Would it matter if he learned where this place was? It might, and at this point his odds for survival looked good. He didn't want to change that. He pulled the blanket over his head and the strong man tied the strap over it, securing his arms. Though this time he only used one strap, and it wasn't quite as tight, which Weasel found encouraging.

"Come along—this way." A large hand descended on Weasel's shoulder and led him off.

"That was an interesting idea you had," his guide added thoughtfully. "About bringing suit. But the teacher, he's right about the political part. You're city-bred, so maybe you'd know. How would most of the townsfolk react if the Hidden sought t' become legal-like? I mean the people, not those Dialan-accursed priests."

Weasel frowned, for Dialan was the month that had just passed—but it seemed more important to answer the question. "People pretty much believe what the priests tell them. About that kind of thing, at least." Was there a chance he could reach this man? "But it was a priest who told me about you, and he said most of the priests agreed that there hadn't been a proven case of your people sacrificing anyone for over two hundred years. As long as you really aren't sacrific—"

His guide laughed bitterly. "If he's lying about that, then he's prob'ly lying about the rest of it as well."

"He's not a liar," said Weasel, stung.

"Then he's a fool. We've never sacrificed any—Well, one man, once. But that was over a thousand years ago, and he volunteered. Except for him, we never sacrificed anybody. But it seems no one's going t' believe that, not city folk."

"If you never sacrificed anyone, why does everyone say that you did?" Weasel asked. "There's no smoke without some fire."

"Oh, there was fire, all right," said the man. "The fire of Boraldis' lies."

"Who's Boraldis?" Weasel asked.

"The god of lies. Or more exactly, of the spirit of lies, and malicious mischief."

"So no one was actually lying? Just some malicious *spirit* persecuting you. I see."

The grip on his shoulder tightened, but Weasel didn't think it was deliberate.

"King Regalis lied," said the deep voice coldly. "Is that name enough for you? The city king, they called him, for he was the city's darling. So him being a liar isn't so surprising, is it?"

"Ah, a malicious old king just woke up one morning and decided to persecute you. I see."

"The Hidden were leading the rebellion against him," said the deep voice. "That's why he lied, for an excuse to make our teachings illegal and hang any teachers his guards could capture. Hundreds, maybe thousands, hanged. The great harrowing, we call it, and the warning was the great harrow, in the constellation of the fish. Which is ironic, because the fish signifies opportunity, and there was no opp—"

Weasel didn't care what the fish signified. "Why did you rebel against the king? I thought country people supported the king."

"Not that king," said the strong man. "Or any king since, though the portents now . . . Never mind. We wouldn't support any king who was robbing honest farmers to the point where they couldn't even feed their own."

Weasel stumbled and the hand on his shoulder steadied him.

"So this king, Rega-whatsit, he just woke up one morning and decided to rob the farmers?" But Weasel's voice wasn't as sarcastic as before. This man seemed to be talking about something more real than gods and portents. Justice Holis had never mentioned a widespread rebellion of farmers against the crown, but the justice tended to focus on current affairs.

"Well, in fairness to him, the city folk were said to be . . . no, they *were* starving," the deep voice admitted. "A bit over two hundred years ago, there were several years of drought, bad drought, all in a row. Nothing we did, no appeal to any god, made a difference. Which was probably a sign in itself," he added thoughtfully.

"A sign of what?"

"We have our guesses. Especially now. But it would be treason to say it aloud, even today. I won't burden a boy with that."

Weasel considered pointing out that he was neck deep in treason, but ancient signs interested him even less than modern ones. Real history, however . . .

"With all the droughts, there was less food, right?"

"Of course there was less food! Even a city boy should know that."

Weasel ignored the insult, for a chill premonition gripped him. He could guess where this was going. "So the farmers stopped sending food to the city. You left us to starve."

He could feel the sigh through the hand on his shoulder. "The farmers sent what they could spare. Or so I'm told, and I believe it. At least, most would. But no man will see his own children go hungry, even if he'd like t' feed others. There wasn't enough. And of course prices rose and rose, so the city rich could afford to eat, but the poor . . . There were riots. And instead of stopping the rich from hoarding, instead of ordering the market brokers to lower the price, King Regalis sent his guard into the countryside to *take* food. A third from every farm. From the silos, and cellars, and even our larders. And there wasn't enough! They were cutting into the seed stocks. The farmers, the whole of Deorthas, was decades recovering, even after the rains came back. When they started taking next year's seed, that's when we rebelled. We knew what it would mean for the land—for everyone, not just the farmers. But we weren't armed men, any more than we are now. The guard hanged so many teachers that half our knowledge was lost with them. That's why . . . Well, never mind. But that's when our faith was proscribed, and why. Nothing to do with sacrifices. Except for the sacrifices the country made, so the city might eat."

"I'd be more impressed by that," said Weasel, "if there weren't people going hungry in the city to this day."

"There may be," said his guide, "but it's not the farmer's fault. Once the rains returned, and the harvests came back to normal— or near normal, for no field in Deorthas is as fertile as it was before Regalis took the throne. Anyway, once the rains returned, things settled a bit. The king who came after Regalis decreed that the farmers need only send a tenth of their crop to the city. But they had to pay for its transportation out of their own pockets, and sell it for no more than they charged in their own village, so it came out closer to a quarter than a tenth. The city tax, they called it."

There were cobbles under Weasel's feet now, and the smoke and dung smell of a village leaked through the blanket. He didn't have much time.

"All right. But that happened centuries ago, and—"

"The city tax is levied to this day."

"Yes, I can see that you're all starving. That's not what this is about."

"What do you mean?" The hand on his shoulder turned him in a new direction.

"You had a reason for dragging me out here tonight. It wasn't because I wanted to talk to you, and don't feed me a lot of rubbish about shooting stars and tests. You had a real reason. What is it?"

They walked in silence long enough that Weasel feared his question would go unanswered.

"We care about the king," said his guide finally. "A true king, wearing the crown of earth once more."

"You mean Prince Edoran?" Weasel snorted. "If you're relying on him to help you, then you'd better take me to the Falcon. He's not interested in helping anyone."

He had bought Weasel two weeks, though. But he could have pardoned all of them, if he'd had the courage. Or cared enough.

"Not yet, perhaps. But if he becomes—"

"Becomes what? Being crowned isn't going to turn a spineless brat into a man."

"The teacher left the choice in my hands," said his guide abruptly. "You've been honest with us. Offered what you could. So I'll offer what I can in return."

"You know where the Falcon is? You'll take me?"

"If I knew where the Falcon was, I'd tell the guard," said the deep voice firmly. "He may call himself a rebel, but I've seen the bodies of coach passengers he and his men have killed. For nothing but the contents of their purses and pockets. Forget the Falcon, city boy. The guard is after you."

"What? How could they be after me?"

Unless they hadn't fallen for the rope hanging out of the tower window. Unless Gabbo had reported seeing them.

"Gossip spreads." The deep voice sounded cheerful. "It's a troop of twenty men, they say, looking for a fourteen-year-old boy with a city accent, and a girl about the same age with chestnut hair."

"Rot!" Weasel whispered.

"Well put." The hand on his shoulder drew him to a halt. "They're about a day and half behind you, but they're mounted, so they'll travel fast. Most folks won't help them. Not tracking down kids your age. But you told half the countryside where you were going, and there's always some that can be bribed. They've got bribe money, too," he added. "They're spending it free, for once."

"I'm surprised everyone they talk to hasn't pointed them straight at us!"

"Not in the country," said the deep voice. He released Weasel's shoulder. "We haven't much use for the guard, not since the harrowing. But they're after you, and if you keep on the west road . . ."

"They'll catch us in days." Weasel shivered, and it wasn't from the cold. If the Hidden hadn't warned him, he wouldn't even have known he was in danger till it was too late.

"Thank you, Master . . . Goodman . . . Goodman?"

There was no answer. He reached out, turning carefully in a circle, but there was no large, warm body within reach.

Even with a looser strap, it took several minutes to struggle free of the blanket. When he was finally able to look around, Weasel found himself in the tavern yard, right outside the privy, where this wild night had started. The cold breeze ruffled his hair. There was no one in sight.

CHAPTER 7

THE FOUR OF WATERS

The Four of Waters: choice.
A decision made, for good or ill. A new path taken.

7

"You should have woken me up!" Arisa exclaimed. "The Hidden! And I missed it!"

Weasel had already explained, several times, that he hadn't been able to wake her, so he ignored this. "The Hidden were a waste of time. I think they really don't know how to contact the Falcon. Three days—lost!"

"They weren't a complete waste of time." Arisa gestured to the small road they now strode along, avoiding the deeper puddles as best they could, since there was no walking path beside this lesser byway.

They had left Sweetsprings that morning, on the main road west, while Weasel told Arisa about the previous night's adventure. By mutual consent, they took the first road to the south that looked like it went beyond the local fields.

"With any luck, the guards will pass through several villages before they figure out that we've changed direction," Arisa went on. "When they finally realize that no one's seen us in the last . . . four villages, let's say, they'll know we left the road sometime after Sweetsprings, but they won't know where. And there weren't many people in the taproom last night, and we didn't call attention to ourselves by trying to start gossip. If they don't question the tavern keeper—or if he decides not to betray us— they'll only know that we left it after Huckstable. As long as we don't call attention to ourselves, they shouldn't be able to follow us."

"But we wasted *three days!*"

"You already said that," Arisa told him. "And I'm not sure they've been wasted. I mean, what else could you do?"

"What I should have been doing from the start," said Weasel bitterly. "I let Father Adan talk me into trying the safe way. Safe, hah! I've gone soft, that's the problem."

"They didn't kill you," Arisa pointed out. "So maybe it was safer. I hope your current plan isn't tramping up and down the roads till the Falcon's men rob you. Father Adan was right about that, and your Hidden friend, too—there are lots of bandits out there who aren't rebels. You could get shot before you even find the bandits you're looking for."

"Of course I'm not going to do that," said Weasel. At least, he wasn't that desperate yet. "It was a stupid idea in the first place. I'm going to work with someone who's sensible—my kind of people. We're heading for the coast, aren't we?"

"Sure."

"All right, then, smuggler's daughter. Where's the nearest coastal town that's in or near the Falcon's territory and big enough to have some real crime?"

It took them a day and a half to reach Coverton.

"You don't have to come with me," Weasel told Arisa, when she complained about the loss of time. "Isn't your mother going to worry about you?"

"Not yet," said Arisa. "My business was supposed to take at least a week, and maybe two."

"Yes, but this isn't like the Hidden. I don't need your help to contact criminals."

Arisa snorted. "You'd need help to . . . ah . . . "

"Yes?" Weasel asked politely.

"Never mind. Let's just say that I don't like Pettibone. If your justice can do something to stop him, that's worth a few days' work."

Weasel frowned. "The conspiracy's been exposed. Most of those men are probably going to hang. Justice Holis can't do anything to stop the regent now."

"He'll still have some contacts that weren't exposed. And even if he doesn't, helping him is the right thing to do. Unlike some people, when I see my clear duty, I do it!"

She proceeded to nag Weasel about his duty on and off throughout the journey to Coverton, until he finally silenced her by pointing out that she couldn't do anything without his help. Arisa's mother was a respectable seamstress who'd fallen into smuggling as a sideline—she had no other criminal contacts. But Weasel understood that real criminals, in a city, knew each other. Even if they weren't road bandits themselves, they would know someone who was. Or know someone who knew someone, and surely the road bandits would all know each other.

The difficulties were first, to find some criminals, and second, to convince them to trust Weasel enough to talk. But he had a solution for both problems.

Coverton was much smaller than the city, of course, but the rattle of wheels and the sound of shouting voices echoed off the stone and brick in the manner to which Weasel was accustomed. It even had the familiar city smell: smoke, rotting garbage, and human sewage. Unfortunately, in Coverton these homey scents were almost covered by the overpowering reek of dead fish.

"We're on the coast," said Arisa, when he complained. "This town prepares and salts the catch from over twenty miles of coastline. What did you expect?"

"The city's on the coast, and it doesn't stink of fish unless you're right on the docks," Weasel objected.

"The city's got lots of other industries," said Arisa. "It's different."

"I'll say."

But Coverton wasn't so different that Weasel couldn't recognize the right kind of pawnshop when he saw it. No jewelry in the windows, nor pocket watches. Nothing more expensive than used clothing and dishes.

"In here," said Weasel, darting through the door.

There was one customer in the shop, an elderly goodwife, who was arguing with the buxom woman behind the counter over the "simply outrageous" price she wanted for a pair of cushions. The firmness with which the pawnbroker held to her price made Weasel even more certain he was in the right place. If this shop was honest, she'd have been desperate to make the sale.

As it was, the customer went off, still puffing indignantly, without the cushions.

"Withless cheapskate," the pawnbroker grumbled. "She could have paid twice the price." She summoned up a smile. "Are you here t' pawn, sell, or buy, m'dears?"

"None of those," Weasel told her. "I'm looking for work."

The practiced smile vanished. "I run the place myself, and I don't need help. Get on with you, boy. There's no work here."

"I'm not talking about *steady* work," said Weasel. "I could get that anywhere. I need a bit of coin to take me down the road. More than a bit, if I can get it."

"I don't know what you're implying," said the woman stiffly. "This is an honest shop, and I'm an honest woman. So you might as well go back . . . to wherever you're staying."

"Where are we staying?" Weasel asked Arisa.

"The Toad and Thimble," she said. "I've been there before. They'll give us loft space for a few chores, and meals for a few more. Though if a bunch of criminals come there looking for us, they'll have us out on the street before—"

The pawnbroker's eyes narrowed.

"Thank you, Mistress," Weasel said swiftly. He grabbed Arisa's arm and pulled her toward the door. "We won't take any more of your time."

"My time's free," the woman told him. "And if the Toad and Thimble kicks you out, try the Empty Net. It might work out for you."

"Thank you," said Weasel sincerely.

The woman smiled. "If it does work out, remember me."

"The Toad and Thimble *will* kick us out," said Arisa as they moved on down the street.

"Then we'll sleep in a church," said Weasel. They'd already passed several churches of the One God. It felt odd to see them outside the city, though Father Adan had told him the One God's faith was gaining acceptance in the larger towns. But the farmers driving their carts down the road seemed comfortable here as well. Perhaps because they weren't forced to sell anything here and could charge whatever a customer would pay. Justice Holis had told him that the towns were growing, and this was a real town, not a glorified village. There might not be quite as many people as you'd see on a similar street in the city, but they walked briskly, not stopping to smile or wish anyone good day. Weasel felt right at home, except for the smell of fish.

"Besides," Arisa went on, "what makes you think that woman knows any criminals? All the things in her shop were household goods. Not the kind of thing a bandit would bring in."

"The owner of a shop like that would starve, selling nothing but household things," Weasel told her. "Folks won't pay much for used clothes and pillows—well, you saw that woman walk out. A pawnbroker's got to handle at least some valuable stuff."

"There wasn't anything valuable in that shop," Arisa protested. "And that woman wasn't starving—far from it."

"So what does that tell you?" Weasel asked patiently.

Arisa stopped, staring at him. "That she keeps the valuable stuff out of sight. Behind the counter, or maybe in a back room."

"And why would she keep her good stuff hidden, where customers can't see it?"

"Because the local guard might have seen a description of it, on a list of stolen goods?"

"Exactly," said Weasel. "Any pawnbroker with his fancies out is either an honest man or a good enough jeweler to have changed them so they aren't recognizable."

He found another pawnbroker a few blocks over, who also had no fancies on display. This one was careless enough to smile slyly when he told Weasel he had no work and then extracted the name of their inn.

"Why are you doing this?" Arisa demanded. "You surely don't think some criminal is going to offer a couple of total strangers a job."

"Depends," said Weasel.

"On what?"

"On whether they've a job in mind that needs a few more hands. We don't exactly look like city guardsmen, you know."

"It's the town guard here."

"Do we look like town guardsmen?"

"No," Arisa admitted. "But I still don't believe they'd just offer us a job."

"Well, they'll ask for some sort of reference first," Weasel told her.

He came to a stop, staring into the window of another pawnshop; it held several bits of jewelry, a handful of silver watches, and two of gold. Not too hard to modify, if a man had the skill.

"What happens when they ask for a reference?"

"I give them one," said Weasel absently. "Let's try this place."

A man sat behind the counter, neatly mending a scrap of lace. That delicate touch might well belong to a jeweler.

"Can I help you, m'boy?"

"I hope so, Master," said Weasel. "I'm looking for work."

The man's polite smile faded. "I've all the help I can use," he said.

"Ah, but I'm not looking for *steady* work. Just something—"

"Get out." The pawnbroker rose from behind the counter as he spoke. His touch might be dainty, but his shoulders were broad. Arisa was already scampering for the door, but Weasel held his ground.

"I'm just looking for a bit of coin, to see me down—Hey!"

The pawnbroker grabbed Weasel's collar with one hand and the waistband of his britches with the other. Weasel's toes scrabbled on the scuffed floor as the man hauled him to the door, then tossed him into the street. The cobbles bruised his knees.

"Ow!"

Arisa knelt beside him. "Are you all right?"

"More or less." Weasel rose to his feet and limped a few steps. His knees ached and his palms stung, but nothing was broken or bleeding. "That's what happens when you come across an honest man."

The last of the sunlight was fading when Weasel peered into an alley and saw the sign for the Empty Net. With any other building, Weasel would have said it "stood" at the end of the alley, but the Empty Net crouched instead, a dark sprawl in the shadow of the taller buildings around it. Light was already glowing in its windows, but instead of offering welcome, it reminded Weasel of a cat with half-closed eyes. It certainly looked like criminals would drink there.

"Not a very nice place, is it?" Arisa's voice was calm.

"Why don't you wait here," Weasel suggested.

"Why should I? I'm your bodyguard, remember?"

"I thought you were my guide."

"Whatever."

She followed him down the darkening street to the door, and though he hated to admit it, he was grateful for her company.

A blast of pipe smoke, voices, and laughter greeted Weasel when he opened the door. But when he and Arisa stepped inside, half the conversations stopped abruptly and then resumed in a murmur.

Most of the customers seemed to be watching Weasel, as he wove through the tables toward the bar. The floor under his shoes was sticky with spilled drink, and Weasel resolved never to eat there. In his lean days, he'd eaten in worse places.

"What're you here for, boy?" The tapster had several days' beard stubble on his chin, and what looked like a full year's worth of stains on his apron.

"I'm looking for work," said Weasel boldly. He'd said the rest of it so many times today that he hardly needed to think about the words, so he concentrated on looking calm and tough as he continued. He hoped Arisa was doing the same. He shouldn't have brought her here.

"We're staying at the Toad and Thimble," he finished, "if you hear about anything."

"I don't run errands," said the tapster indifferently. "You want work, come back."

Weasel's heart leaped, but he kept his voice even. "Does that mean there's a job for me?"

"No." The tapster's grin revealed several broken teeth. "It means I don't run your errands."

A burst of laughter greeted the words, and Weasel's cheeks burned. He nodded and turned to walk out—not too slowly, lest they take it as a challenge, and not so fast they'd think he was running. With predators, it was fatal to run. Arisa followed like a shadow.

They were halfway to the door when it happened.

"Here, sweeting," said a drunken voice. "What's a pretty girl like you doin' in boy's kit? You should have a skirt, an' a bodice that shows a bit . . . up here."

Weasel turned just in time to see the drunk's hand run over her breasts.

Grab his hand, yank it back. Then say, "That's my sister," in a cold, deadly voice. The gesture, the words flashed through Weasel's mind. But before he could move, Arisa struck, grabbing not the drunk's hand, but his fingers. She bent her wrist so swiftly that Weasel didn't realize what she was doing till he heard the crack of bone.

The drunk screamed, high and shrill. Cradling his hand, he stared at three fingers, bent at unnatural angles. They were already beginning to swell.

"You broke 'em!" he wailed incredulously.

And she'd done it so fast! No warning, no girlish squeal. Snatch, snap!

Weasel realized that his mouth was hanging open, and he closed it.

Arisa looked around the room. She didn't have to gather the crowd's eyes—everyone was staring. She put her hands on her hips, shoving back the skirts of her coat to reveal the knife.

"The next man who lays a hand on me loses that hand," she said, in a colder, more deadly voice than Weasel could ever have managed.

It should have sounded absurd, but every man in the place, Weasel included, swallowed in unison. She meant it. Worse, she could *do* it.

Arisa strode out of the room, head high, and Weasel hurried after her.

Her arrogant swagger didn't change when they reached the alley, but Weasel noticed that she took several deep breaths. Somehow, it made her human.

"I can't believe you did that!" She'd seemed so sane, so *normal*, traveling with him these last few days, that he'd forgotten about Gabbo and the knife. "Who *are* you?" She was no ordinary girl, that was certain.

"Arisa Benison. I told you that. Several times."

She was beginning to sound like herself again, which almost made it worse. Weasel's voice was still squeaking. He took a couple of breaths and deliberately tried to lower it.

"That's not what I meant." It came out sounding calmer, which made him feel calmer too.

"I know. I'm sorry about messing up your pitch back there," she added.

"What do you mean?"

"Well, they're not likely to offer us work now, are they?"

"Are you joking?" How could she be so terrifyingly competent with violence, and so naive? "That story will be all over town by morning, and they'll be lining up to hire us! It's the best advertising we could get."

Weasel was wrong—it took the next morning, and part of the afternoon, for the tale of Arisa's confrontation in the Empty Net to spread through the town. Several of the pawnbrokers she and Weasel spoke to that day commented on it, and they heard a garbled version from the kitchen girl at the Toad and Thimble while they washed that night's dishes. According to the kitchen girl, Arisa had been a great lady disguised as a road bandit, or possibly a road bandit disguised as a great lady, and she'd gone into the tavern alone.

But in spite of the rumors, and all Weasel's efforts, another day passed before the old man approached them.

Weasel and Arisa had started spending the early evening at the Empty Net, lingering as long as they could over mugs of hot tea. Tea only, since Weasel's resolve not to eat there strengthened each time he saw the place, and neither of them wanted alcohol slowing their responses—not in this tavern.

So Weasel was instantly aware of the old man when he rose

from his chair by the hearth and tottered his way over to Weasel and Arisa's table.

"Buy an old man a beer, m'boy?"

Weasel considered this. The man was far too old to engage in criminal activity himself, stooped and wrinkled, his head completely bald. But Weasel noticed that the wrists sticking out of his ragged sleeves still looked strong, and his pale eyes were keen. He wasn't as feeble as he appeared, or sounded—but he looked so feeble that if Weasel told a panel of justices that this man had tried to recruit him for a criminal job, he'd be laughed out of court. In short, he was the perfect man to make an approach.

"We've barely enough to buy tea for the two of us," Weasel told him. "But the One God teaches that if you look after your fellow man, then he'll look after you. That's right, isn't it?"

The old man's eyes vanished into a mass of wrinkles when he smiled. "I'm not much of a churchgoer, but that sounds right t' me. Least, it might be true. Now and then."

"I'll get it." Arisa started to rise.

"No." Weasel reached out and squeezed her shoulder in warning. "Let me go. You stay here and talk to our new friend."

He managed to stumble as he passed the chair where the old man was seating himself, bumping against him for just a moment—but for Weasel, that was enough.

When he returned to the table, carrying the foaming mug, Arisa was laughing and the old man was speaking in a high, piping voice. "'Oh, la, sir,' I says to him, 'You'll make me blush!' The poor fellow all but burst, trying t' explain to his officer that he hadn't been gropin' my skirts. Skirts is a fine place to smuggle anything smaller than a crate, if a man can pull it off. And you'd have no problem with that. You should try skirts sometime."

"I know," said Arisa. "My mother's said the same. But the truth is, I do better fighting in britches than telling lies in a skirt."

"Besides," said Weasel, setting the mug on the table and taking his own chair, "she'd never be able to say, 'Oh, la, sir' without giggling, or scowling, or something that would give the game away."

Arisa giggled.

"I could do it, though," Weasel added. He lifted his voice to a feminine falsetto. "La, sir. You make me blush!" He batted his eyelashes flirtatiously, and the old man laughed.

"I've got lots of talents," said Weasel. "And I won't ask much for using them, since part of my price is a bit . . . unusual."

"Hmm," said the old man. "Something special you want, is it?"

"Yes," said Weasel. It would have been safer, and easier, to get a job with the gang and then gradually blend into the criminal population of the town. To learn about the Falcon in a series of casual conversations that no one would think twice about. But Justice Holis' trial would begin in a week, and it might not last more than a few days. He was running out of time.

"What would it be you're looking for?" the old man asked.

"First the job," said Weasel. "No point talking about payment if I can't earn it."

"Ah. You understand there's a small matter of references to be covered first."

The man was smiling, like any cheery old gaffer, but his shrewd eyes watched Weasel closely.

"Will these do?" Weasel reached into his own pockets and pulled out the old man's purse, his pipe, his folding knife, and a crumpled handkerchief that was a bit disgusting, but Weasel had filched it anyway.

The man's smile vanished when he recognized the purse. His hand twitched toward his coat pocket, but he stopped the motion with a swift self-control that told Weasel a lot about what his youth had been like. With the smile gone, he was formidable enough to make Weasel nervous—but Weasel too had grown up in a hard school, and he didn't let it show.

"Took 'em off me when you went to get the beer? How'd you know I'd be asking for references?"

Weasel shrugged. "If you'd offered me the job without asking for some proof I wasn't a guard informer, I wouldn't have taken it."

The soft-looking smile came back. "Nice to do business with a clever boy. A skilled one too. I must be getting old, not t' have felt the lift."

"Maybe. Or maybe I'm that good."

In truth, Weasel had gotten rusty in three years of clerking for the justice. He'd been practicing picking pockets, and then putting the items back, ever since he realized he'd have to seek out criminals to assist him. Arisa's purse had been in and out of her pocket a dozen times in the last few days. Weasel hoped she wouldn't figure that out, but the suspicious glare she leveled at him now wasn't a good sign.

"So what's the job?" Weasel repeated.

The old man gathered up his belongings and replaced them in his pockets. He didn't count his money, Weasel noticed. He hoped the gaffer would be amused, rather than annoyed, when he discovered that he'd paid for his own beer.

"They left the decision t' me," he said finally. "And I think you're worth a try. There's a warehouse down by the docks," he went on, as Weasel tried to keep the sudden surge of triumph out of his expression. "Kind of a magical place, this warehouse, for it seems that things like silk and spices just appear there, and no one's ever seen 'em being unloaded at the docks. Of course they all have proper duty stamps, so there's nothing the guards can do."

"And the ink on those stamps is almost dry," Arisa murmured.

"Oh, it's dry by the time the goods goes in," the old man told them. "But the guards are a bit skeptical about this 'appearing' business, so they tend to hang about in the neighborhood. 'Specially at night."

"I guess they don't believe in magic," said Weasel.

"I can't say what they might be thinkin'," said the man. "But the sad fact is, once the sun goes down there's a small army of guards on that warehouse."

"You've got a shipment," Weasel guessed. "And you only get paid on *delivery*."

The old man didn't so much as look at him. "But by day, m'boy, there's not so many guards. Just half a dozen, t' keep an eye on things. Of course, the streets are full of people then, so's it might be hard for folks to get something in without being seen. Unless that something was disguised as something else. Then you could make your move in broad daylight, except for the guards. But those lads would go poking and prying; might even open the crates right up. Unless, of course, someone distracted them while the goods was carried in."

Weasel's heart began to pound. "You want me to lure off the guards? How long would you need to be clear?"

"Fifteen minutes should do it," said the man. "Twenty, t' be on the safe side."

Weasel winced. "Not possible. Bait and run's dangerous for the bait, even for a short time. In twenty minutes they'll either have given up or they'll have caught me. And I can't afford to get caught. I can buy you five minutes clear, maybe a bit over, but I can't guarantee more than five."

"Fifteen," said the old man. "You've got a partner, after all. That should help you stretch the game a goodly bit."

Weasel looked at Arisa. Her face was bright with interest and excitement. She was clearly smart enough to understand what they were talking about, but she wasn't experienced enough to know how hazardous bait and run really was. And the longer the chase, the higher the odds that the bait would be swallowed.

On the other hand, this was the only offer he'd gotten in three days. Justice Holis was running out of time.

"Five minutes guaranteed," said Weasel. "But I'll try for ten."

They finally settled on ten minutes guaranteed and try for fifteen, though both of them knew Weasel was unlikely to succeed.

"So now we got the job set," the man went on, "what's this special payment you're wanting?"

HILARI BELL

"It's information," Weasel told him. "I want coin, too, mind. Five gold blessings for the pair of us. But I also need to contact the Falcon."

"The Falcon?" The old man's brows rose. "What do you want with a road bandit, boy?"

"He's a rebel leader," said Arisa. "Not a bandit."

Weasel scowled at her. "What I want him for is my business," he told the old man. "Do you know someone who could take me to him?"

"Hmm. I can't m'self, you understand, but . . . We could maybe arrange that. But you're not getting five blessings for the job. Not on top of introductions. Five copper flames are enough."

They settled on eight silver stars, two in advance, with the job to take place two days hence. Final payment would follow completion.

By the time they left the Empty Net, Weasel was sweating as if he'd been running races.

"We did it!" Arisa exclaimed as they reached the street. "You've got your job, they'll guide you to the Falcon at the end of it, and I'll have enough money to get home. Why are you looking so grim?"

"Because these are my kind of people," said Weasel. "And I know why he was trying so hard not to pay us up front. I thought I'd never get him to agree, even to the terms we got!"

"I noticed that," said Arisa. "But I don't understand why you care. Of course he doesn't want to pay us too much up front; we might have taken his money and left town. Though knowing how long we've been looking for a job, I'd think he'd believe us.

Especially since it was pretty obvious that an introduction to the Falcon is what you really want."

"Oh, he knew that," Weasel told her. "If it had been straight coin, we'd probably have gotten six or seven gold blessings for this job. If they have a way to approach the Falcon without getting themselves killed, they got a bargain."

Arisa frowned. "Then why did he haggle so hard about paying up front?"

"Because even two stars isn't as good as free," said Weasel.

"Free?"

"If the guards catch us, they won't have to pay anything. That's what they're gambling on. They've got pretty good odds, too."

Fifteen minutes. Ten guaranteed. He must have been mad.

"Arisa."

"What?"

"There's nothing you can do to help with this. And it could be . . . it will be dangerous. I think it's time for you to go home."

Arisa snorted. "It hasn't been dangerous before this? Besides, I'm a better fighter than you are."

"This isn't going to involve fighting." He hoped. "It's a matter of running and escaping, and that's my job, not yours. And don't give me any blather about your duty to fight the regent," he added as she opened her mouth to argue. "The conspiracy's over. Pettibone will probably rule till he dies—the One God help that spoiled princeling—and there's nothing anyone can do to stop him. This is going to be dangerous."

Arisa closed her mouth and thought a moment. "All right," she said finally. "Forget about duty, to your realm, to your people, to your God. Or I suppose you can't forget it, since you never gave it a thought in the first place. Let's say I'm doing it because I owe you."

"What do you mean? You don't owe me anything."

"You got me out of the dungeon, remember? I couldn't get out on my own. You saved me, so I owe you. Just like you're saving Justice Holis because he saved you. Why else are you risking your neck, if you don't owe him?"

"It's not because he saved me," said Weasel. "It's because . . . because . . ."

Because Holis was the first person who had loved Weasel since the mother he scarcely remembered. But that had nothing to do with Arisa. She'd become a friend, yes. The first he'd had in . . . Maybe the first he'd ever had. But she had a mother who loved her, and the other friends she'd talked about, so why was she doing this?

"Why are you doing this?" Weasel demanded.

"Because I owe you."

Weasel recognized that stubborn expression—she would say nothing more. He played his final card. "If we get caught, your mother may be the one who pays the price."

"My mother would agree with me," Arisa told him calmly.

"Then she's as foolish as you are."

But it seemed this fool was now his partner.

"You won't get caught," Arisa told him confidently.

"How do you figure that? The odds against us are—"

"You won't get caught," Arisa repeated. "Because if you get caught, Justice Holis will hang."

CHAPTER 8

THE SIX OF FIRES

The Six of Fires: the traitor.
A trust betrayed, or a promise broken. A spy.

8

Weasel gazed at the guardsmen who lounged on the street in front of the warehouse. Three of them today, and he knew there were four more scattered around the building. Yesterday there had been five, and he wondered why two had been added. Two more men should make no difference in the execution of his plan. *Should.* Weasel wiped damp palms on his britches, even though the day was cool and clear.

He must have been mad to agree to this.

He had no choice.

Coverton's town guards wore uniforms, too, but their coats were a shade of blue that didn't go well with their black tricorne hats. And the bright red waistcoats were downright vulgar.

When he'd told Arisa that yesterday, she asked acidly if he was studying to be a tailor. So Weasel pointed out unpolished boots, missing buttons, and stains that no city guardsman would have tolerated. Arisa scoffed. Patiently, Weasel commented on a number of potbellies, and one man with the reddened nose and cheeks that spoke of a long addiction to bottle and jug. Men who hadn't the discipline to care for their clothes usually didn't keep their bodies in good condition either.

Arisa eyed Weasel's too-large britches and the patched elbows of his coat.

"That's different," he told her. "We've been traveling. Besides, they're your clothes!"

He then spent the rest of the day scouting escape routes in three different directions, proving to her that in his case sloppy clothes didn't indicate a sloppy mind.

But only going east, into the business district that bordered the warehouses and docks, gave them a real chance of keeping those men on their trail for fifteen minutes, so he had stationed Arisa to wait for him on that route. If he could draw them east, he might succeed. Otherwise . . .

The town clock chimed one, the hour the gang had told him to start his diversion.

Weasel studied the people on the street. The woman with the shopping baskets? She couldn't chase him without dropping her purchases, and she'd probably set up a great screech, but she didn't look very prosperous. Would these guards chase a thief for fifteen minutes if they didn't think they'd get a reward? Not likely.

The young man with the silk coat and the lace cravat looked more than merely prosperous—a local shareholder's son, like as not. But he also looked fit enough to run Weasel down without the guards' help, and thrash him with his own two fists into the bargain.

Long minutes crept by as Weasel rejected one possibility after the other. Most people in this area were working men and women; sailors, stevedores, fishmongers. There was nothing in their purses to tempt a thief, and they couldn't afford to reward the guards if they chased Weasel a single block.

Surely someone would turn up. . . . Wait! There. A stout middle-aged man, in an embroidered waistcoat, was coming out of a tobacconist's shop with a parcel under his arm. If his clothes were any indication, he had money, and he didn't look like the type who'd go chasing after a pickpocket.

The gentleman left the shop and started down the street to the west. Perfect. Weasel pulled himself off the step where he'd been idling and followed the man, walking briskly to close up the distance, but not too fast. He didn't want to catch up till they'd passed the guardsmen.

Watching closely, without seeming to watch anything, Weasel saw that the three guards straightened up and smoothed their waistcoats into place as the man approached—though the gentleman paid them no attention. An important man; someone they wanted to impress. Excellent. Weasel might be able to keep them on his heels for fifteen minutes after all.

Weasel waited till the gentleman was well past the guardsmen, but not yet to the corner. Then he darted forward and, *deftly now, deftly*, eased the fat purse from the man's coat pocket. The gentleman walked on, oblivious.

So he hadn't lost his touch. Justice Holis would not have approved, but for once, Weasel didn't care. Sighing for the betrayal of his craft, he tugged gently on the man's coattail.

The gentleman started and spun around, groping for Weasel, who danced out of his reach. The man's purse was plainly visible in his hand.

"Ho! Thief! Stop him! I've been robbed!"

For a gentleman, he had good lungs. The woman with the shopping baskets couldn't have made more noise. Weasel ran for the corner, without looking back to see if the guards followed. If this didn't fetch them, nothing would.

Darting among the startled pedestrians, avoiding those who looked alert enough to make a grab for him, Weasel heard the guards shouting behind him.

"Stop him! Grab that boy! Thief!"

He was smiling as he rounded the corner and ran north, down the side of the warehouse. Only one guard was posted here, looking around as if he'd heard the shouts but didn't yet know what they meant.

Weasel slipped to the other side of the street, behind a dray loaded high with barrels and pulled by a four-ox hitch. He'd passed the guard before the man realized he was there, but the other guards, who were rounding the corner, remedied that.

"Stop that boy! He's a thief!"

The shouts sounded a bit breathless, and Weasel grinned, even as the fourth guard joined the chase. Four down, three more to go. The new guard was closer than the other three, and fresher, too, so Weasel was running hard when he turned the next corner and discovered that the two guards stationed there were more alert than their fellows.

This street was narrower. When they saw Weasel running toward them, they had the good sense to spread out, one on one side, one on the other. It would be hard to get past them if they kept those positions, but that was a big if.

Weasel didn't even slow down. He raced along the side of the warehouse as if he didn't see the guard who swung in to intercept him. And sure enough, as his partner shifted toward the warehouse, the second guard followed, moving into the center of the street and then past it.

Weasel looked up and started, as if noticing them for the first time. Then he changed course, as if he intended to run between them. Both guards leaped to intercept him, bumping into each other. Weasel zigged sharply to the center of the street, passing just out of reach of the farther guard.

This maneuver left the two guards right behind him, forcing Weasel to put on a burst of speed. He was breathing harder now, and he might not have managed it if not for the sudden surge of fear. Being captured by guards was the first part of the nightmare that ended in his hanging.

He was only a few yards ahead of them, but the distance was growing. He had almost reached the corner of the warehouse when the final guard came out to investigate the commotion.

He wasn't supposed to join in till he saw the others run by! But he'd appeared early, and there was no help for it. At least he wasn't entirely certain of what was going on, though he was alert enough to stand in front of Weasel and hold out his arms.

"Halt, in the name of the—"

No time for finesse. Weasel bent down, raising his arms to protect his head, and ran into the guardsman's stomach like a battering ram. When the guard doubled over and fell, Weasel ran right over him and off down another street . . . toward the east.

A swift glance over his shoulder showed him that the men in the lead had paused beside their fallen comrade. In fact, it looked like one of them had tripped over his body and fallen as well, so Weasel allowed his headlong pace to slow.

He could use a breather, and he had no fear that these plump old men could overtake him. The difficulty would be holding them to the chase for fifteen minutes—they'd probably burst their hearts if they ran that long. On the other hand, if they began to gasp and slow, they shouldn't be too suspicious if he slowed down as well. They were already too winded to shout instructions at passersby.

And Weasel had other tricks in store.

The first of them was Arisa, who was now trundling a barrow-load of dirty laundry down the street toward him.

Weasel gave her a cheerful wave as he jogged past. He'd gained enough distance that he felt entitled to turn and watch the next act.

He'd guessed that she'd have good timing. Arisa over-turned the barrow right in front of them, bringing down both of the lead guards—one tangled his feet in the tumbling cloth, the other caught his shin on the barrow as he tried to leap over it.

Arisa started running the moment the barrow fell. Weasel had time to wait for her while the guards clambered, cursing, to their feet, and the men behind them worked their way around the obstacle.

"Good job!" he exclaimed, as she raced past him. She gained

half a dozen yards before she realized he was running much slower than she was and fell back to join him.

"Not so fast," Weasel told her, as they sprinted on together. "They're getting tired. It's too soon . . . for us to shake them."

He was a bit winded himself—clerking really was making him soft, curse it. But the building where he'd planned his main delay was nearing, and he could run that far.

Looking back, he judged the distance and decided it was about right. He signaled for Arisa to go ahead of him, and she raced for the tree that stood next to Weasel's "really good idea, honest!" and scrambled into the branches with the speed and agility of someone who'd practiced it several times. In the dark, too.

She was halfway up by the time Weasel reached the base, and by the time he hauled himself into the branches after her, she was crawling along the branch that stretched to the roof of the leatherworker's shop.

If it had been summer, with the tree in leaf, they might have lost their pursuers at this point—though the people in the street, who'd stopped to stare, would probably have given them away. But in late Moran, with all the leaves gone, anyone could see them. As Weasel crawled out on the branch, he heard a breathless shout: "Look! On th' . . . roof!"

By the time the branch began to sag, the low railing that skirted a flat section of the rooftop was within easy reach. It still took a bit of nerve to transfer his grip from branch to railing and let his body fall against the building's wall. If he hadn't practiced it, he might have hesitated. But he and Arisa had returned to this building after dark, when the streets were almost empty and the shop deserted, to make certain his plan would work. Now she reached down and helped him drag himself onto the roof, which made it even easier.

Weasel peered over the edge.

Seven sweaty, red faces looked back at him, frustrated, furious. Even if they were willing to make the climb, the branch he'd used would never support their weight.

Come on, figure it out. I haven't got all—

"Hey!" one of them cried. "We've got them trapped! Spread out and surround the building."

Weasel pulled his head back and sat, leaning against the railing. He needed a rest—now he could get it.

"How long do you think it'll take them?" Arisa was still looking down.

The sound of pounding boots told Weasel the guardsmen were moving.

"Five minutes," he said. "First they've got to surround the building—and that's tricky." The leatherworker's shop might have started as one small building, but as the business grew it had expanded to encompass a number of neighboring shops, connected by covered alleys and yards, some of which had been walled in and some of which hadn't. From the ground, it was almost impossible to tell where one building ended and another began.

"Then it has to occur to them that there's probably a hatch to get up here," Weasel went on. "And judging by what I've seen, that'll take longer than it should. Then they have to convince the shop owner that they really do have a desperate villain trapped on his roof. At least five minutes. And at a slow walk, which is the best pace they'll be able to manage afterward, it's almost five minutes back to the warehouse. We'll give our employers fifteen minutes, easily."

"Maybe we should get the ladder ready," said Arisa. "Just in case."

That wasn't as easy as it might have been. Only parts of the roof were flat; the rest was a frozen sea of peaked slopes, at odd angles, and the slates were slippery beneath his boots. But in a few minutes they had the ladder ready to go, and from where they stood they could see the trapdoor that led onto the roof. Anyone who came through it could also see them, but this was the only place they could be certain of wedging the ladder in securely. You couldn't have everything, Weasel told himself philosophically. They'd been incredibly lucky as it was.

They'd found the ladder, lying against the back wall of a neighbor's warehouse, when they'd first scouted the area. It had inspired Weasel's "really good idea," for it was long enough to cross the narrow street from the leather shop to the much-flatter roof of the warehouse next door. And as he and Arisa had discovered, propping one end on a rain barrel and the other on an abandoned crate, it was sturdy enough to hold both of them at once. With practice, they'd learned to cross it quite quickly. It hadn't even been too hard to get it up on the roof, though that proved noisier than he'd liked.

When they reached the other side of the roof, Weasel looked down. One of the guards, already looking up, shouted, "There! There he is!"

Weasel stepped back from the edge. "A master of the obvious if ever I heard one. We have to wait till they open the trap door before we lay the ladder across."

Arisa snorted. "And that's not obvious?"

Weasel grinned. "All right, it is. But you've got to admit, it's going pretty well so far."

"I admit it. Actually, I'm impressed. How did you know how the guards would react?"

"I'm pretty good at reading people," Weasel told her. "A pickpocket has to be. So does a lawyer. Justice Holis says that people are all that matters. I'm beginning to think he's right, though I use my knowledge of people more . . . profitably than he did."

"He sounds like a good man," said Arisa. "But soft."

"He's not soft," said Weasel defensively. "All right, he is, but that's . . . Never mind. I like soft in a justice. Particularly one who might be judging me."

"Your law-clerk coating is beginning to wear thin," Arisa told him. "The pickpocket's showing through. Shouldn't they be coming through that trapdoor?"

"Any minute," Weasel confirmed.

A minute passed. And another. Another. By the time the hatch banged open, Weasel had begun to think they'd given up and gone, but the guardsman's face that appeared in the opening was as triumphant as he'd expected.

"Got you!" the man shouted. Then he saw the ladder and swore.

"Now," Weasel murmured. He and Arisa swung the ladder in a controlled fall over the alley. It ended in a not-so-controlled crash, but this was no time to fret over details.

"Go!" Weasel cried, and Arisa started scrambling across the ladder toward the next roof.

The guard was still heaving himself out of the hatch when Weasel started after her. The view from the ladder to the alley floor would have been terrifying if he'd had time to be frightened, but the guard had emerged from the hatch and was climbing over the slippery slates. If he reached the base of the ladder before they got across . . . If he was angry enough that he'd rather see them dead than escaped . . . Weasel was all but crawling on Arisa's heels when she rolled off the ladder and onto the warehouse roof. And she hadn't been slow.

Weasel scrambled to safety and spun around.

"Watch out below!" he shouted, and shoved the ladder off the edge.

It made a horrifying crash, but looking down, Weasel saw that the guard still stationed there had taken his warning to heart and gotten out of the way.

He grinned and ran after Arisa, who was already on the other side of the warehouse roof. The side that faced the docks, where the big crane rested, its ropes trailing all the way down to the street. To escape.

Fortunately, no one was using it now—though the crane

ropes were only one of several ways Weasel had found to descend from the warehouse. The fastest way.

"After you," he told Arisa politely.

Her face was alight with excitement as she grabbed the rope, wrapped her boots around it, and slid swiftly down. Weasel wondered again about her past. He knew why he'd learned to climb from a tree to a building, and slide down a rope, but she was a seamstress' daughter!

This wasn't the time to speculate. Weasel twisted his ankles around the rope and slid down, just slowly enough to avoid burning his hands.

Several people on the street were staring, but no one moved to stop them. Weasel smiled at them and took Arisa's arm, setting off at a brisk walk. With any luck, they'd have disappeared before the guards even—

"Halt, in the name of the law!"

"Run," Weasel commanded, and set the example. He'd delayed them for fifteen minutes already—there was no reason to hold back now. The cobbles flew under his racing feet, and Arisa ran beside him. They'd give up in just a minute. Any time now. But the thundering boots behind him weren't growing fainter.

He glanced back over his shoulder. The three men who chased him wore town guard uniforms, but their faces weren't familiar, and the lean bodies in those uniforms belonged to younger men. They were running easily, at the same pace he was. And they hadn't run a chase already this morning.

"They're not . . . the same ones," Arisa panted. "Got . . . reinforcements."

Alarm raced through Weasel's veins, but he was already running as fast as he could. This was why they'd been so slow getting up to the roof! The exhausted guardsmen had sent for help. For someone who was fit enough, fast enough, to chase a couple of kids over a rooftop. And they'd just had time to get down through the leather shop and around to the warehouse before he and Arisa escaped.

"Come on!" Weasel grabbed her arm and swung her, skidding, down a side street toward the docks. The chaos there might give him a chance to lose them.

He yanked a crate of chickens off the top of a stack as they ran by, but the crashing crate, the sudden burst of clucking, flapping birds, barely slowed their pursuers.

He had looked at the guardsmen's girth and underestimated their intelligence. He'd been arrogant. He'd been stupid, in a way that Weasel-the-pickpocket never would. And if he didn't get lucky, he was going to pay the price.

The bushel of potatoes he cast across the road delayed them no more than a moment, though Weasel heard one of them swear as his feet rolled out from under him.

The wagon he and Arisa darted under, when it blocked the road, gained them a bit more time—they were shorter, and flexible enough to keep their feet as they scrambled under the wagon's wide bed. The guardsmen were forced to drop to their knees and crawl, but they didn't hesitate to do it, and the distance Weasel and Arisa gained wasn't enough.

He wondered again why she had taken this risk. She'd be regretting it now.

Weasel's breath came in gasps, and a muscle in his side was beginning to cramp. He couldn't run much longer, and the guards behind them showed no sign of tiring. He fought down a surge of despair.

It was then that Arisa grabbed his arm and dragged him into a narrow side street . . . leading up a steep hill.

Weasel's feet slowed. "Can't!" he wheezed.

But a shout from his pursuers proved that he could, and he drove his aching legs upward.

Through vision blurred with sweat and exhaustion, Weasel saw that they were trapped. There were no side streets off this hill, no alleys, not even a narrow gap between the buildings. The only way out was at the top. His lungs fought for air and couldn't find enough.

Arisa grabbed his arm as he stumbled, pulling him up, and up.

The guardsmen's boots echoed in the confined space.

Weasel tried to run faster and couldn't. Not even for Justice Holis. Not even the thought of capture and hanging could push him farther.

When Arisa let go of his arm he fell to his hands and knees, head bent. Colored lights swam in the darkness behind his eyes. He felt sick. He would have passed out if he'd dared, but the guards were still coming.

Over the thunder of his own pulse, he heard a series of wooden clacks and thuds. He opened his eyes and looked.

Arisa crouched behind a wine keg that lay on its side, ready to roll. Her face was hard and intent as she twisted the barrel, aiming it with the concentrated intensity of a master gunner bent over his cannon. Then she gave it a push.

It didn't roll straight. A barrel's curved surface isn't designed to roll in straight lines, and the uneven cobbles sent it bouncing this way and that as it crashed downward. But it was heavy enough, and the hill was steep enough, that it picked up speed quickly, and its unpredictable course was to their benefit. It swerved at the last second, into the shins of a guard who had stepped to the side, hoping to avoid it, and sent him flying like a toppled tenpin.

He sat up, clutching his leg, and when one of his comrades spoke to him he shook his head.

"Got one!" Weasel gasped. He wanted to laugh, but he was panting so hard he thought laughter might kill him. Still, the surge of delight brought him to his feet in time to help Arisa lift the next keg off the pile.

The two guardsmen who were coming up the hill eluded that one, and they put on a burst of speed after it passed. If a slow, upward stagger could be called a burst. They looked to be almost as winded as Weasel, but they were still climbing.

"Two at once!" Arisa commanded, sounding like the master gunner Weasel had dubbed her.

"Yes'm," he said, and stole a second to snap off a crisp salute.

Two kegs, rolling down together, were almost impossible to avoid. One man crammed himself into a narrow doorway at the last minute. The other leaped desperately over the first barrel only to land on the second, which rolled him down and then rolled over him. He stood up after it had passed, but slowly. And his companion waited for him before going on.

The man with the injured leg had found a slightly deeper doorway and was standing there.

Weasel and Arisa sent the next two kegs rolling down, and when both of them missed they launched the next pair, and the next, and the next. The man who'd lit on the barrel was knocked down a second time, and when the remaining guardsman finally fell, three barrels rolled over him before he could regain his feet. One keg took a lucky sideways bounce and knocked the man with the injured leg out of his doorway. He limped down the hill as fast as he could, peering back over his shoulder.

His surrender decided the others, who turned and ran, clinging to the buildings and avoiding the tumbling kegs as best they could.

Arisa harassed them with ongoing fire, but used only one keg at time, so the guardsmen managed to elude most of them. Weasel wanted to cheer, but he was too busy catching his breath to waste any.

When the guardsmen finally vanished around the last of the buildings, he actually managed a slow jog down the street that led them away.

"That was brill'ant, that bit with the kegs," the old man chortled.

The crowd at the Empty Net had greeted them with a cheer

when they walked in that evening. Weasel was starting to feel right at home there—it was definitely time to move on.

"That was Arisa's idea," Weasel admitted. "And it was. Brilliant, I mean."

Arisa blushed with embarrassed delight, like a girl being complimented on her ball gown. "I saw the kegs stacked in the alley and thought it might work."

"Well, it did," said the old man. "And so did your plan, m'boy. Was over twenty minutes 'fore those guards came back to the warehouse, and by that time the goods was in and we was out. No way for them to prove what we carried wasn't legal. They didn't even try."

"So you'll be paying us," said Weasel firmly.

"Yes." The man heaved a sigh. "I've no choice, for you surely did the job. Come along with me."

He rose and tottered out of the tavern, acting even older tonight than he usually did. Weasel might have felt sorry for him, but by now he was fairly certain that "acting" was the proper word in every sense.

"Where are we going?" Arisa asked, looking around the dark street uneasily. "Why couldn't you pay us in the Net?"

"The coin, I could have," said the old man. "If I was carryin' it. But for the special part of your payment, you've got t' meet your guides. So I figured I might as well pay all at once. We're here, anyway."

"Here" was a dilapidated warehouse. Not surprising, since this was a district of warehouses, and other businesses that served the docks, but something about it made the back of Weasel's neck prickle. And judging by Arisa's worried expression, she felt the same.

"Why couldn't we meet them at the Empty Net?" Weasel asked. Or any other well-lit, public place. Not a sliver of light showed beneath the door the old man was unlocking. He snorted.

"These are road bandits, boy! Sketches of their faces are tacked to the courthouse door. With rewards posted under 'em. You're lucky they agreed t' meet with you."

The door swung open. A couple of small windows cast squares of moonlight on the floor inside, making the shadows by the walls even darker. Weasel heard the soft rustle of cloth, a scuff of leather on wood, that told him men lurked there.

Oddly enough, that reassured him. A road bandit, in a town where he was wanted, would avoid the light. He followed the old man into the room, Arisa coming after him.

"Close the door," the old man said. "I'll light the lamp."

Arisa hesitated for a moment before she turned and did as he asked.

The click of the latch was followed by the rasp of a striker. The sudden flare illuminated the old man's wrinkled face and the lamp in his hands. Then the lamp's wick caught and light welled out, touching the men who stood in the shadows.

Four men, wearing the green and white uniforms of the palace guard.

Weasel cried out, in furious betrayal.

Arisa didn't waste even that much time. She ran at the nearest guard before he could move, ramming her head into his stomach. He doubled over, just as the guardsmen beside him reached out and grabbed Arisa's arm and shoulder.

Weasel, frozen in the incredulous paralysis that always held him when she did something like this, saw her boot heel rise and then smash down on the guard's foot.

Bone snapped. Weasel was wincing even before the man screamed.

"For the God's sake, she's only a girl." The voice was an officer's, cool, impatient. "Grab her and hold her!"

Weasel didn't move. It was the first law of hiding in shadow—in any place, really. The human eye is drawn to motion.

The old man looked at Weasel, then his eyes went to the fight. Clearly, he felt his job was done. Bastard.

The guard with the broken foot was on the floor, clutching it, swearing. But the third guard was moving behind Arisa, and the other was straightening up.

"Draw your truncheons and take her!" the officer snapped.

"But sir, she's . . . she's a *girl*."

They didn't want to hit a helpless female. Weasel fought down a hysterical urge to laugh.

Arisa drew her knife.

The guards were armed for patrol, with clubs instead of pistols. And she was still a girl. They hesitated.

"Oh, for—" The officer pulled his truncheon out of his belt, stepping forward, and Arisa turned to face him. He swung at her shoulder, a solid stroke that would have broken her collarbone had it connected.

Arisa darted to the side and then in, slashing the officer's arm with her blade. Blood spurted, scarlet in the glowing light.

At the sight of blood, the guards' training kicked in. This wasn't a girl, but an enemy. The one on Arisa's right grabbed her wrist, twisting till she cried out and the knife fell. The other swung his fist at almost the same moment, crashing into her temple. She dropped limply to the floor.

"About time," the officer snarled. He clutched his bleeding arm.

No one was looking at Weasel.

Two long, silent steps took him to the door, and he opened it and fled, slamming it behind him. It wouldn't delay them more than a second, but in the dark, in a neighborhood where he had learned the streets, Weasel had no doubt he could elude them.

But then what?

CHAPTER 9

THE THREE OF FIRES

The Three of Fires: the lost messenger.
Important information missing or unknown.

9

How could I have been so stupid!

He'd known the old man's gang didn't want to pay them. What better way to avoid it than to turn them over to the guard? They probably earned a reward! The Hidden had told Weasel that the palace guardsmen were spending bribe money—they'd have put out posters, offered a reward, as soon as they realized they'd lost Weasel's trail. Why hadn't that occurred to him?

Because he was stupid. Because he *had* gone soft, working for Justice Holis. Not only soft in body, soft in the head. Soft in his heart. He had to be hard now. To be ruthless.

That resolve faltered instantly, for the first act of a ruthless man would be to abandon Arisa.

Weasel sat down on a darkened step and rubbed his face wearily. He'd eluded the guard even more easily than he'd hoped, turning a corner and then squirming into a narrow gap between two buildings. A grown man couldn't have fit in that narrow slot. Weasel had only to wiggle into the deeper shadows and hold still—the guardsmen had run right by.

Only two of them, the man with the broken foot and one other, had stayed to guard Arisa. But that had gained Weasel nothing, for two trained fighting men could take him out with ease. As easily as they'd finally taken her out, once they got over their shock.

In fact, Weasel realized, the reason she'd previously beaten opponents who were so much larger and stronger was mostly because her willingness to fight took them by surprise. Didn't she know that?

Of course she did. She probably relied on it—but this time, in a drawn-out fight against four men, it had failed her. It would fail in any fight that lasted more than a few minutes—and she must have known that as well. So why had she attacked them?

Because if she hadn't, they'd both be prisoners now. She'd worked with Weasel enough over the past week to know that if she created a diversion, he'd use it.

But she was relying on him to rescue her. Which made her almost as stupid a chump as he'd been. Weasel had *told* her that the criminals in the Empty Net were his kind of people. And they were. What an idiot he'd been to trust them. She knew he had to rescue Justice Holis, too. Every day he spent trying to free her lessened his chance of finding the Falcon in time. Lessened his chance to save a man whose chances were too slim already.

His eyes stung and he pressed his hands against them. Pressed back the memory of a warm study, and a laughing voice telling him he had "no social conscience."

Fools. Both Arisa and the justice. Marks for the plucking.

And Weasel was worse than either, for he knew better. He had just resolved to be hard, and ruthless, and survive. . . .

He sighed and rose from the step. If he was going after Arisa, he needed to change his appearance—those posters would carry his description. Perhaps even a sketch. As for Justice Holis . . .

Maybe some miracle would draw the trial out for a few days. As he walked down the dark street, looking for an apothecary to rob, Weasel gave some thought to learning to pray.

There was no sketch, and the description tacked to the court-house door fit half the fourteen-year-old boys in Deorthas. As a pickpocket, Weasel had already learned that common brown hair and eyes were a blessing. All he had to do was darken his hair with walnut stain and change the one thing that made him stand out—his city accent.

He'd been listening to enough country folk lately that he could probably fake their speech patterns. A backyard laundry line pro-vided a new set of clothes, rougher and more patched than Arisa's. The worn kerchief he tied round his neck completed his transfor-mation. Now he had to find, or create, a chance.

Weasel stationed himself beside the town gate early the next morning, with a floppy-brimmed hat and a stolen basket of apples that he was offering for sale. He wanted to make cer-tain—he couldn't afford to lose them—but he thought the guards would linger in Coverton for a few days trying to capture him. Those days would give him time to plan Arisa's rescue. But with the way his luck was running, he wasn't surprised when they rode up to the gate two hours after sunrise.

Surrounded by other peddlers, Weasel watched from under the shelter of his hat and wondered why they were leaving so soon. Did they think he was too smart to try something so foolish?

Too smart to remain in the town where he'd almost been caught? They thought he was smart. . . . Clearly they didn't know him very well.

Whatever the reason, they were departing this very morning, and it looked like they intended to travel fast. There were packs on their saddles, and the man whose bandaged foot dangled free of the stirrup led a couple of packhorses behind him.

The other three surrounded Arisa, who sat on her horse straight-spined despite the livid bruise that covered the left side of her face. Her wrists were bound to the saddle in front of her, and they'd tied her horse's lead rope to the officer's saddle.

She held her head high, but Weasel, watching closely, saw her eyes searching the crowd. He wanted to draw her attention, to give her some signal, but he didn't dare. If one of the soldiers noticed, he could end up right beside her, and there would be no escape for either of them. When she was free, he could apologize. When she was free, she wouldn't care.

They set off through the gate at a brisk walk. A walking man could keep up with a walking horse, but it was tiring, and sooner or later Weasel would have to get ahead of them—which meant he needed a horse of his own. Thanking the One God for the purse he'd lifted yesterday, Weasel set off to lease himself a mount.

Justice Holis had insisted that he learn to ride, so Weasel had, but he didn't like it. And as he soon discovered, there was a world of difference between the iron-mouthed brutes the livery stable rented and Justice Holis' sweet-tempered mare.

"Pull his head around," the stableman shouted. "Once he

knows you won't take any nonsense, he'll go fine for you!"

Unfortunately, the big gelding didn't want his head pulled around. Despite Weasel's tugging, kicking, and swearing, the gelding turned and went back into the stables, then into his own stall. Weasel managed to duck in time to avoid being brained on the door frame, but it was a near thing.

"You withless, bone-headed brute!" said Weasel.

Choking noises emerged from the stable boys, some of whom were younger than Weasel. The stable master sighed.

"Saddle up Bessie," he told one of the smirking youngsters. "We'll have t' reduce his fee, but if we don't put him on Bess, we'll never get him out of the yard. She's the gentlest mount we've got," he added, turning to Weasel. "We keep her for . . . ah, riders like yourself."

"What's so wrong with Bessie, that you'd have to reduce my fee?" Weasel asked. "So old she can barely hobble? A children's pony? She'd better not be a cow!"

"Only at heart," the grinning stableman told him.

In fact, Bessie was a plump, amiable-looking mule. Weasel eyed her suspiciously. "I thought mules were stubborn."

"Some are," the stableman admitted. "But Bessie's not. She may not be as fast as a horse, but she can travel longer."

Thinking of the two hours the guardsmen had already gained, Weasel sighed.

"She'll carry you anywhere you want t' go," said the stableman encouragingly. "And she's gentle enough to carry your granny, though your granny prob'ly . . . Any stable that serves the Swiftline coaches can see her back to me."

Your granny probably rides better than you do.

He might be right, at that. "I'll take her."

Bessie proved willing to carry him, and she cost less than a horse, both in terms of the lease per day, and the amount he left as security against her safe return. She was also fond of apples, sneaking several from his basket before Weasel persuaded her away, so he sold the basket to the stable master and set off down the road with only a small pack. And if riding to the rescue on a mule wasn't exactly heroic, well, Weasel wasn't exactly a hero, so he shouldn't care.

The purse Weasel had filched contained a couple of gold blessings, and enough stars to pay for Bessie's rent and allow Weasel to eat and sleep at the finest inns between Coverton and the city, so money was no longer a problem.

Unfortunately, catching up with his quarry was. Weasel rode through luncheon, stopping only to buy himself a bit of bread and a handful of dried fruit, and it was still past dark when he reached their camp. A real camp, with a fire in the center, and tents set up in a patch of woodland between two fields.

Weasel rode Bessie right on by, paying them no more attention than a mildly curious glance. He was fairly certain that none of the guards had looked closely at him—they'd been too busy with Arisa. Still, there was no point in taking chances.

He wondered why they'd chosen to camp, instead of staying in town. Perhaps they knew how much easier it would be for him to reach Arisa in a nice, crowded inn. Or perhaps they'd paid out so much money in rewards and bribery that they could no longer afford it.

But Weasel could. The next coaching inn was less than a mile down the road, and Bessie's weary steps quickened when she recognized a familiar stable.

The stable boys recognized her, too, and their sidelong glances mocked Weasel for riding an "old granny's" mount. The covert glances changed to outright laughter when Weasel swung himself out of the saddle and collapsed to the ground. His legs ached from the tips of his toes to halfway up his back. His muscles were so wobbly that even with one of the snickering boys helping him, it took him several attempts to get to his feet and stagger into the inn.

The innkeeper's wife was sorry to hear that his mother was so sickly he'd had to leave his job as a merchant's clerk and go home to assist her. She drew him a bath, for a few coppers, and gave him some muscle ointment from sheer mercy. Either that, or she didn't want to cope with a guest who was crippled for life.

Weasel wasn't sure if it was the bath or the salve, but he was able to get out of bed the next morning and limp down the stairs to the common room. He'd already begun his meal when the guardsmen brought their prisoner into the inn for breakfast.

So they weren't staying at inns, but they were eating there. Hmm.

They showed no interest in their fellow diners. In any case, Weasel, wearing a combination of the clothes he'd stolen and those Arisa had given him, looked more like a village boy, eating at the inn for a treat, than a traveler on the road.

Arisa spotted the coat before she recognized him, which reassured Weasel about his disguise. Aside from the widening of her eyes when she confirmed that it *was* him, she showed no sign of recognition and didn't look at him again—smart girl.

Weasel was able to watch them fairly closely. In fact, it would have been suspicious not to watch, for half the room was staring. And muttering comments that the guards couldn't hear, but Weasel could.

It seemed that dragging a poor young girl—what could a girl that age have done?—off to prison, flogging, or wherever she was being dragged off to, didn't sit well with the country folk. And no matter what she might have done, they didn't have to keep her hands tied up like that. Surely four big, strong men could handle one girl.

Weasel suppressed a grin.

The guards took themselves off as soon as they'd eaten, before one man had even finished his tea. Being the focus of that many glares had to make for uncomfortable digestion.

Weasel gave them a few minutes' start, paid his bill, and went out to mount Bessie. She looked fiendishly fresh this morning, even prancing a bit as the stable boys brought out her tack. Weasel mounted, wincing, and set off down the road.

The ride wasn't quite as bad today, for he was able to stop for meals when the guardsmen did, though he didn't go into the inn where they ordered luncheon. They hadn't seemed to notice him at breakfast, but seeing a familiar face might make them look more closely. Fortunately, there was a bakeshop across the street where he could eat a pork pie and peer through the inn's windows without making himself conspicuous.

Even from a distance, the hostility of the inn's other patrons was obvious. The common guardsmen looked more and more uncomfortable as the meal went on. The officer's face was expressionless, but his spine was ramrod straight.

Perhaps that was something Weasel could use.

Since Arisa had recognized his coat that morning, he found a shop that sold used clothing and bought himself several coats and hats, suitable for different incomes and professions.

Dinner at the next inn was a repeat of their earlier meals. Weasel wondered if the guardsmen rode out of town to camp because they feared that if they stayed, some sympathetic country-men might offer to aid the girl.

When Justice Holis had spoken of the countryside's hostility to the city guardsmen, Weasel hadn't believed it really mattered. The king had the army, after all—the discontent of a bunch of bumpkins could hardly be significant. But after watching the guardsmen drag Arisa through hostile towns for just one day, he was beginning to understand that the country folk could make a difference. A big one, if they became angry enough to act.

Weasel, somewhat less stiff than he'd been the night before, took a room at a smaller inn and went to find the local apothecary.

She too was sympathetic about his mother's inability to sleep in a strange bed, and readily poured out the four doses of sleeping syrup he asked for. But when he mentioned his notion of mixing the syrup with a glass of wine, she absolutely forbade it. Alcohol would increase the power of the dose, possibly to a lethal degree, and the stronger the drink, the worse the danger. No, no, just a teaspoon mixed in with a glass of water, or a nice mint tea if the bitter taste bothered her. No alcohol with the potion, or for at least six hours beforehand.

Weasel told her anxiously that his mother had drunk a mug of ale with her dinner, but that was over three hours ago, and ale wasn't nearly as strong as wine. Couldn't his mother take a dose tonight? After several days in the rocking coach, and no sleep, she was mortal tired. . . .

The apothecary sighed and allowed that ale, particularly drunk with food, was probably safe, though she told Weasel to halve the dose. In fact, some of her poorer patients were permitted to mix the potion with ale, but if they did that it was to be no more than two or three drops in a mug, and that dosage wasn't as sure. . . .

Weasel walked back to his inn, whistling. He would have to leave early in the morning to get ahead of them.

The sun was still an hour from rising when Weasel dragged himself out of his warm bed and went shivering down to the stables. He'd paid his tab last night and told them he wanted to leave very early, so the night groom was ready to saddle Bessie when he arrived. Weasel, who had donned one of his respectable coats this morning, had a story prepared about a wealthy aunt, who had a habit of changing her will, suddenly taken sick. But the groom showed no interest in his early departure.

The sun still hadn't risen, but the sky was going gray when he rode past the meadow where the guardsmen had camped. The cold gave Weasel plenty of excuse to pull his collar up, and his tricorne hat down around his ears. And giving the camp a look as he passed by was the most natural thing in the world.

They'd set up two small tents and another, slightly larger, for the officer—only three tents for four men, because one of them, clearly posted as a sentry, sat beside the fire wrapped in a blanket and sipping something that steamed in the fresh morning air.

It took Weasel several seconds to locate the mound of blankets beside a tree where Arisa was sleeping. He looked away, fighting down a surge of indignation. They had another tent available! They could have pitched it for their prisoner.

On the other hand, kindness to prisoners wasn't a guardsman's duty. How fitting that their lack of consideration would work to Weasel's advantage. If he'd had to search through the tents to find her, it would have greatly increased his chances of rousing someone.

He gave the camp a final glance and saw that the sentry's curious gaze had dropped from Weasel—in his perfectly adequate disguise—to Bessie. Bessie, who had passed this camp several days ago, with someone of Weasel's size and shape riding her.

The man's expression showed no recognition, as far as Weasel could tell. He didn't cry "halt!" or raise an alarm, so he must not be too suspicious. People riding mules down country roads weren't too unusual. Even if he could identify Bessie—and to Weasel, she looked just like every mule he'd ever seen—two sets of travelers passing each other on the road wasn't uncommon.

Still, it would be foolish to let them see Bessie again. If their prisoner suddenly vanished, if that guardsman remembered the mule that seemed to be following them, they might go looking for that mule.

A Swiftline coach pulled into the small village just as Weasel reached the inn. While the grooms changed the sweating horses for a fresh team, Weasel paid the driver for a seat and then arranged with the stable to see Bessie back to Coverton. He bid her farewell with a reluctance that surprised him, but a city law clerk didn't need a mule, and money was money. A note for the remainder of the security he'd paid the stable master would arrive at Justice Holis' house at some later date . . . if Justice Holis still had a house, and if Weasel was there to receive it. Only two days till the trial started. Could he possibly find the Falcon in time? But he couldn't abandon Arisa—once she was locked up in some city cell, he'd never be able to free her. It was sheer chance that the dungeons had been full, forcing the regent to resort to the makeshift cell they'd escaped.

Weasel pushed those thoughts aside. His fellow coach passengers might notice if he spent the whole trip fretting. In fact, the coach was half empty. The other seats were occupied by two sisters, traveling together to visit their brother, and a stout man with rough hands who smelled faintly of onions. Once they'd greeted Weasel, the sisters returned to their conversation—they never stopped talking—and the man went to sleep. Though how he could sleep in the bouncing, rocking coach was a mystery.

It would be ironic, Weasel thought, if the Falcon's men robbed this coach. They were still in the area Arisa had described as his territory, though they were approaching its border.

If the coach was robbed, Weasel would seize the chance! He had to; he was running out of time. If he could persuade the road bandits to take him to their leader, perhaps he could persuade the Falcon to rescue Arisa as well as Justice Holis.

That was a lot of persuasion, so Weasel spent the next few hours preparing speeches for a variety of people and situations. Unfortunately, the coach continued without incident, and Weasel, who had long since learned the difference between fantasy and reality, made a final purchase in the town where they changed horses midmorning. He might not have thought of it, but the traveling tinker who'd opened his pack in the inn's courtyard carried some very well-made kitchen knives. The one Weasel finally chose was smaller than the one Arisa had taken from Gabbo, but it would cut through the ropes far more swiftly than his penknife, for the tinker had honed it to a razor edge.

By midday, Weasel had learned enough about their route to guess that the soldiers would stop at the same town as the coach for their luncheon. He was even more certain that they would camp near the same village where the coach pulled in for the night, since it was five hours' journey to the next town after that. They were running behind when they pulled into the inn yard, shortly after midday. But the Growing Grape, accustomed to missed schedules, offered the passengers a luncheon of hot meat pies they could eat as they traveled onward.

Weasel pleaded exhaustion, and the driver gave him a chit that would let him continue his journey on the next Swiftline coach—assuming they had a seat to spare.

The servant who brought out the pies had returned to the kitchen, and the grooms were too busy harnessing fresh horses to pay any attention to Weasel as he slipped into a shadowed corner of the yard and swapped his enough-money-to-afford-coach-fees coat for one of the patched ones. He waited till the coach had been gone for several minutes, and the grooms had returned to the relative warmth of the stable, before he sought the taproom. It smelled of cooking meat and beer. Weasel's stomach growled, but he waited till the woman behind the bar had finished serving several other customers before approaching her.

"What can I do for you, m'boy?"

"Please, m—goodwife, may I speak t' the innkeeper?"

"You're speaking to the innkeeper. I inherited this inn from my own mother, and I'm not inclined to share."

"I'm sorry," said Weasel, trying to keep the satisfaction out of his voice. He hadn't dreamed he'd be lucky enough to find a woman owning the inn. "M'master told me I had to talk t' the man in charge to purchase a cask. He's camping outside town with the carts, but he sent me in t' buy food and ale for him and the rest."

Was his accent too thick? But if he was from a distant village it might be thicker, or slightly different from theirs. The woman didn't look suspicious.

"Have you a kettle to carry something hot back to them?" she asked.

Weasel shook his head. "They said you'd pack things up for me."

She frowned at this and he added hastily, "We've got soup on the fire back at camp. It's just, we're all mortal tired of Edom's cooking."

She laughed, accepted Weasel's copper flames, and sent a man off to the cellars for a small cask. While they waited, she gathered up a bundle of the hot pies that hadn't sold to the passengers of the half-filled coach, along with roast potatoes, and some berry tarts that made Weasel's mouth water. He had to swallow before he spoke.

"I'm grateful t' you, for takin' all this time. Busy as you'll be with the guardsmen and all."

"Guardsmen?" she asked absently, wrapping a handful of pickles in oiled paper.

"They don't seem t' be here yet," said Weasel, thanking the One God for that with all his heart. "But we passed them on the road not far back. Heard about them before we passed them too."

The woman frowned, looking at him for the first time since she'd started working on his request. "How could a string of carts pass a party of guards on horseback? They are riding, aren't they? We haven't room for a company of foot soldiers."

"Oh, they're riding," Weasel assured her, as he scrambled for an explanation. The arrival of the serving man, who set the cask on the bar with a thump, gave him a few more seconds.

"I guess they're going a bit slow 'cause of their prisoner. Be hard on a girl, riding dawn to dark. Nice girl, they say. Just turned fourteen . . . 'fore it happened."

No one could have resisted that bait. "What happened?"

"She killed her stepfather," Weasel told her, with the gruesome relish with which some folks speak of murder. "Hit him on the head with a fire iron, and then kept hittin' him and hittin' him. They say she had good reason, by most folks' reckoning."

He lowered his gaze, as if ashamed. A well-brought-up country boy shouldn't speak of such things.

The woman's mouth tightened. "He was abusing her?"

"From the time her mother died, when she was nine," Weasel confirmed. "Or so she says. 'Course, her stepfather's kin says different, and it's her word against theirs."

"But why would she lie, why kill him like that, if he wasn't doing something to deserve it?" the woman asked indignantly. "They're taking her in for that? Wait, why didn't this go to court in her town?"

"It did," Weasel improvised rapidly. "And the local justices acquitted her. Self-defense, or justifiable homicide, or some such thing. But th' stepfather was a friend of the shareholder. Or maybe he owed him money. Anyway, the shareholder went t' the regent, and now she's going t' be tried in the city, by a panel of justices the regent's going to pick. Or so they say."

"Lady bless us!" the woman exclaimed. "I never heard of such a shameful thing."

Weasel nodded. "I heard that some guards turned it down. That they had a hard time finding men who'd volunteer to fetch her in. Folks along the road are upset about it. I'm told that half the inns they ride into are refusing them service, since they don't let the girl eat with them, but only their own. . . . "

A clatter of hooves in the yard announced the timely arrival of the guards. Looking through the taproom windows, Weasel saw Arisa, bound to her saddle. Strands of dark red hair, pulled loose from her braid, framed her plain, freckled face. She looked more like a tired farm girl than a murderess.

Angry red stained the woman's cheeks.

"Here's your bundle, m'boy," she said grimly. "Excuse me. I have something to attend to."

She took off her apron and straightened her cap, then stalked majestically out of the taproom, like a galleon under full sail— gun ports open. Weasel had several things to do, and not much time, but he couldn't resist listening to the opening salvo.

"Bring those horses back here," she commanded in a carrying voice. "These . . . *men* aren't staying."

Weasel grinned. He picked up the cask and his bundle and hurried down the corridor and out the back door that led to the privies. Then he made his way quietly around the side of the inn. He didn't need to look around the corner to know what was going on.

The officer's voice was very stiff. "Mistress, I know the girl looks innocent, but she—"

Weasel stowed his bundle of food under a nearby bush and worked the bung out of the cask. The rich smell of beer greeted him.

"She was *found* innocent, you withless pig," the inn's mistress proclaimed. "By a panel of justices in her own town."

"She was?"

Weasel, pulling the sleeping syrup from his pocket, heard the baffled note in the officer's voice. But after several days of glares and muttered insolence, this insult was the final straw. The officer's hard-held annoyance buried the questioning tone so deep that only someone listening closely could have heard it. The crowd would only hear . . .

"You've even got the gall to admit it!" the innkeeper exclaimed. "Well, you'll find no shelter under my roof! Dragging a girl who was only defending herself off to be hanged!"

A hostile growl, from what sounded like the beginnings of a good-sized mob, greeted this remark, and Weasel risked a glance. There weren't as many he'd thought—less than twenty men and women gathered around the guardsmen. But the anger on their faces made up for their small number. Arisa sat silent on her horse, her gaze lowered and her cheeks scarlet. The watching country folk probably took that for shame at her situation. Weasel suspected she was struggling not to laugh.

He uncorked the sleeping syrup and hesitated. The apothecary said only three or four drops to a mug, but that was for a sleep aid, not to make a man sleep so deep he couldn't be roused. There were four teaspoons in the little bottle. How many mugs were in this cask? Ten? Twenty? Thirty? How many drops in a teaspoon? Weasel didn't want to kill the guardsmen—they were only doing their jobs.

"I don't know where you came by your information," said the officer. "I myself don't know what she's been charged with. But my duty is—"

"I heard you volunteered to bring her in," the woman growled.

"Like a girl her age could be guilty of anything worth arresting her for, much less hanging her!" a man's voice added indignantly. "In the old days, when the king had the sword and shield beside him, a man could count on justice. Nowadays—"

"It wasn't the sword and shield made the king," a woman told him. "It was the crown of earth! Not that the city kings have that, either. And Regent Pettibone doesn't for sure!"

The nonsensical argument reminded Weasel of the Hidden, quarreling over their portents, but the crowd rumbled agreement.

By the scent of it, this batch of ale was fairly strong. The apothecary said the amount of alcohol was what magnified the effect. Weasel took a deep breath and poured half the sleeping syrup into the cask. He corked the bottle and put it back in his pocket.

"I know she's young," the officer said grimly. "But I assure you, she is not what she appears."

"And how would you know that?" a different woman demanded. "You said you didn't even know what she was charged with! How do you know she's guilty?"

The crowd growled again, louder.

Weasel found a rock and pounded the bung back into its hole. Under most circumstances he wouldn't have dared do it so quickly, but the crowd, on the brink of becoming a mob, made enough noise that the hollow thuds were lost.

Weasel didn't think the officer would admit that one slim girl had almost outfought his men. And the mob probably wouldn't have believed it, anyway.

"I see there is no point arguing with you." The disdain in his voice brought forth another growl. "Clearly, you are open to neither justice nor common sense. We will depart now, but when we reach the city, we'll see what our commander says about an inn that refuses to serve officers on the king's business!"

Perfect! Weasel had hardly dared hope for a threat. He peeked out, just in time to watch the officer wheel his horse around, scattering the crowd, and ride out of the inn yard. His men tried to look equally proud and indifferent, but the nervous way they scanned the faces around them undermined their efforts.

Weasel didn't blame them. A city crowd might have thrown stones at this point, but the country folk were less violently inclined—or perhaps the handful of villagers who'd been caught up in this affair weren't the troublemaking kind.

Weasel let the guardsmen get a minute's start, then he picked up the cask and ran after them.

The street was busy enough to slow their horses, so he caught up with them a few blocks from the inn.

"Sirs," he gasped, for the run had left him short of breath. "Stop, sirs, please. M'master wants t' apologize. Please!"

The officer gave him a single, arrogant glance, but he pulled his horse to a stop. The other three looked at the cask.

Weasel's newly dark hair clung to his sweaty face, but it

would be better if they were listening to his country accent instead of looking at him.

"The master of the Growing Grape sends you this cask of fine ale in the hope that you'll forgive the i'pertinence of his wife," Weasel announced, in the half chant of someone repeating a memorized message. "He didn't mean no disrespect, and if he'd known what was happening he'd have stopped it."

"It would seem," said the officer frostily, "that your master has little control over his establishment, or his wife."

"Well, that's the truth, Goodman, ah, sir," Weasel admitted. "I don't know why he thinks he could've stopped it, for he never can, not when Mistress has the bit between her teeth. Proper harridan, she is. But he did send me t' bring you this ale. It's the good stuff, too," Weasel went on, confidingly. "Nothing cheap. Mistress will skin him for it, when she finds out."

The soldiers laughed, and the officer unbent enough to smile.

"We accept your master's apology."

"And no need t' go mentioning this t' your commander?" Weasel asked hopefully.

"That depends," said the officer. He kicked his horse into motion.

"'Pends on what?" Weasel asked.

The soldier who took the cask from him winked. "Depends on the quality of the ale."

Weasel watched them ride out of town. He hadn't dared look at Arisa, but surely she'd know better than to drink that ale— assuming she was offered any, which he thought unlikely.

If the guards accused the inn's proprietor of taking a hand in their prisoner's escape, the simple fact that she had no husband should make it clear that someone else had managed the affair. Once the full story came out, all she could be blamed for was falling victim to Weasel's lies, which the soldiers had done as well. Her spirited defense of the innocent would do her no harm.

Weasel turned and made his way back to the inn, reclaiming his bundle of food and his basket. He had plenty of time now.

Walking steadily, Weasel came in sight of the camp shortly after darkness fell. They had chosen a clearing in a small copse of trees—judging by the blackened fire rings, it had been used for this purpose before.

Out of reach of the firelight, too far off to be heard as long as he didn't make a lot of noise, Weasel tucked himself under a thick bush and dined on cold meat pie, potatoes, pickles, and two of the berry tarts.

Watching the firelit camp was like watching a stage from the darkened rear of a theater. The troopers set up their tents, cooked a simple meal, and allowed their prisoner to eat before they gave her a handful of blankets and bound her to a tree. Weasel frowned, for the tree was too far from the fire for him to see exactly how they did that, but it probably wouldn't matter.

Only after the camp was ready for sleep did they broach the ale.

Weasel watched them drink. Had he made the dose too strong? He had no desire to poison four men. But *your honor, I*

didn't mean for them to die. Honest. He could all but see the justices' sneers.

Surely it wasn't too strong. Even if alcohol amplified the effect, he'd only put two teaspoons into the whole cask.

Had he used too little? If the sentry didn't fall asleep . . . Or even worse, what if someone woke when Weasel was in the midst of freeing Arisa? His imagination supplied the feeling of heavy hands descending on his shoulders and a rough voice exclaiming, "Got you!"

In fact, this whole journey could be an attempt to lure him into the open! But if that was true, surely they'd have recognized him when he offered up the cask, despite different clothing and hair. No, he was imagining things. He went right on imagining them until the yawning troopers finally sought their tents. Until the sentry, whose head had been drooping for the last half hour, lay down by the fire and began to snore.

Weasel waited another half an hour, until the waxing moon began to rise, before he paced quietly down the road and, even more quietly, into the guardsmen's camp.

A couple of men were snoring, so he probably hadn't commenced his career as a mass poisoner. He'd have been happier about that if the sentry beside the fire hadn't muttered something and rolled onto his side as Weasel approached. The man had turned his face away, and his snoring resumed as soon as he settled, but Weasel's heart continued to pound.

Yes, the sentry had fallen asleep, but it seemed to be a normal sleep, not nearly as deep as he'd hoped.

Oh, well. There came a point in any lift where you had to grasp the mark's purse—to commit yourself to the job and get on with it. Weasel eased himself between the tents, one step at a time, testing to make sure there were no snappable branches buried in the grass. The grass rustled softly, but Weasel thought he was making an astonishingly small amount of noise . . . until he drew near the tree and met Arisa's critical gaze.

He raised a finger to his lips for silence, and she rolled her eyes in exasperation. *Like I don't know that?*

Weasel suppressed a sigh. He should have known that three days' imprisonment wouldn't turn her into a tearful puddle of gratitude. And while he was delighted to do without the tears, a little more gratitude wouldn't have hurt.

When he was a few feet away, Weasel drew the knife, prepared to cut whatever ropes held her.

Arisa grimaced again and sat up, shedding her blankets so slowly that not even a whisper of moving cloth broke the silence. Her hands and arms were free. Only one ankle was shackled to the tree, with a padlock securing the chain.

So much for the knife.

Weasel thanked the One God that he hadn't fallen so in love with respectability as to obey Justice Holis' irrational whims, stuck the knife quietly into the ground, and pulled out his lock picks.

Arisa smiled, but she still didn't allow her ankle to so much as twitch—the chain hadn't clanked once.

Weasel appreciated her self-control. If she moved, the drowsy soldiers would probably assume she was turning in her sleep, but any sound might rouse the sentry, and if it did . . .

Weasel had just knelt to examine the shackle's lock when he heard a rustling sound and Arisa's fist thumped on his shoulder.

He didn't even turn to look, scrambling as quietly as he could behind the tree. He could hear Arisa drawing the blankets over herself, a soft whisper of fabric.

He heard the scrape of a canvas flap falling into place, and stumbling footsteps. His heart raced and his eyes sought some path through the trees. Could he hide among them if he had to evade pursuit? He should have used the whole dose, curse that soft, stupid conscience Justice Holis had foisted on him! Would the man only chastise the sentry for falling asleep? Or would he take the sentry's place? If they compared notes about how sleepy they felt, if they realized the ale had been drugged, and started looking around . . . The knife! He'd left it sticking in the ground in front of Arisa, and if that wasn't enough to give them away . . .

He heard the liquid hiss of a man pissing and risked a glance. The soldier was standing some distance from the camp, with his back turned. The knife was gone. Arisa must have snatched it into the blankets when she covered herself—smart girl!

But there was no way to conceal the fact that the sentry was asleep.

I'll wait till he's yelling at the man, then I'll run, Weasel decided. The guard's attention would be fixed on his erring comrade, and the loud voices ought to cover any sounds Weasel might make, but the brush around the camp was so thick that someone running through it would sound like a charging cow. And even if

Weasel made his escape, even if they didn't suspect the ale, any-one posted as sentry for the rest of the night would do his utmost to resist the drug. The syrup had made them sleepier than nor-mal, but it hadn't knocked them out.

Weasel bit his lip in frustration, waiting for the man to notice the dozing sentry . . . but he never did. Unsteady footsteps took him back into his own tent, and cloth rustled as he settled him-self. A few minutes later, another snore was added to the chorus.

The syrup might not have knocked them out, but it had fogged their minds. He still had a chance.

Weasel came out from behind the tree and sat beside Arisa, but he didn't start working on the lock right away—you can't pick a lock when your hands are shaking.

Arisa gazed at him curiously. *Drugged?* Her lips shaped the word without a sound.

Weasel nodded.

Ale? she mouthed. Weasel missed most of the rest of the sen-tence—he wasn't an accomplished lip-reader—but the words for "you" and "cask" were distinctive, and he nodded again.

Respect dawned in her expression. Was this the first time he'd seen it? If so, he should complain! He'd done plenty of good, smart work over the last week. Still, his breathing slowed and his hands finally steadied.

He lifted the blanket gently, trying not to disturb the chain, and set about picking the lock. The small snap when it opened made him flinch, but none of the snores even paused. Arisa's ankle showed raw patches where the steel had rubbed. She pulled her foot from his grasp and donned her stockings and boots.

No one showed any sign of waking, so Weasel rose and made his way through the camp. It was tempting to turn in to the shelter of the woods, but it would be too noisy, and too dark, despite the rising moon. He picked his way between the tents as quietly as he could, with Arisa a shadow at his heels. She made less noise than he did, he noticed. But if she could have moved faster than his snail's pace, she betrayed no impatience.

Concentrating on his feet, Weasel had cleared the last of the tents before he realized that Arisa was no longer behind him. He spun to look back.

She stood over the sleeping sentry, right next to the fire, and the knife blade flashed as she turned it. Her expression was detached, calculating. She looked at Weasel, gestured to the guard, and made a swift, slashing gesture. *Shall I cut his throat?*

Weasel shook his head. *No!*

She scowled. She walked two fingers across the air. Then all her fingers scurried along the same path.

Weasel frowned incomprehension, but he kept shaking his head to make sure she got the message. *Don't do it.*

She pointed the knife at him, then to herself, and walked the two fingers again. Then she pointed to the road. *The two of them, escaping.*

Even as she waved her knife at the tents, Weasel understood the rest of it. *If I kill them, they can't follow us.*

Weasel felt the blood drain from his face. The crazy cutthroat meant it! She was going to kill four men so they could make a clean getaway.

Weasel couldn't shake his head any harder. He opened his mouth in a silent scream, then clamped his right hand over his left wrist. *One yell, and we're caught!* He waved her forward, urgently. *Come here, right now!* He wished he had a signal to add *you lunatic* but his expression probably conveyed that part.

Arisa frowned, as if someone had insulted her craftsmanship. She held a finger to her lips and gestured with the knife across her own throat. I *can do it quietly.*

Perhaps she could. Weasel was no longer certain what this madwoman could and couldn't do, but it was also possible that she wasn't as good as she thought she was. And even if she was that deadly, these men didn't deserve death.

Weasel didn't know how to sign "Over my dead body." He started toward her, back to the most dangerous part of the camp, which he'd already passed through twice. *You stupid, bloodthirsty . . .*

His expression must have revealed his determination, because Arisa sighed and tucked the knife into her belt. Then she gestured for him to stay where he was and walked toward him, silent as a passing breeze.

He grabbed her wrist when she reached him, ignoring her silent snarl, and drew her firmly down to the road. The packed earth made no sound under their feet, but Weasel didn't break into a run until they were several hundred yards from the camp.

They ran till they were both gasping for breath, and too far from the camp for anything but a shout to reach the sleeping guardsmen. The live, sleeping guardsmen—no thanks to her!

"Why did you stop me?" Arisa demanded. "They'll start hunting us as soon as they wake! And I have to say, whatever you drugged them with, it wasn't strong eno—"

"You lunatic!" Weasel managed to keep his voice low, but it was a near thing. "You were going to kill those men! Just on the *chance* they might be able to catch us. You're mad. You're absolutely, raving mad. Who in the One God's name do you think you *are*?"

Her face was serene, her voice calm, but he saw laughter in her eyes. "I'm Arisa Benison, just like I told you. But my mother is the Falcon."

CHAPTER 10

THE SEVEN OF STONES

The Seven of Stones: the woman.
A gathering of women. A woman's power.

10

"Your mother's *what*?"

"My mother is the Falcon," Arisa repeated. "I'll take you to her now. It will take a while to get there, but—"

"You'll take me to her *now*?" Weasel's voice rose incredulously. "Do you mean . . . You could have taken me to her from the start! Do you mean to tell me we didn't need the Hidden? We could have skipped that mess in Coverton? We could have saved weeks! You lied to me!"

"Be quiet!" Arisa hissed. "You'll wake up the guards. I don't take strangers to my mother."

Weasel tried to lower his voice, but it wasn't easy. "I'm not a stranger! I was in jail with you!"

"*Pettibone* put you into that cell with me," Arisa reminded him coolly. "A cell from which you, conveniently, knew how to escape. And the first thing you did was declare your intention of looking for the Falcon! Not to mention how often you said you didn't care about the rebellion, didn't care who ruled, didn't care about anything but your friend and your own precious skin! Pettibone didn't know who I was, but he knew the buyers were linked to the Falcon. He could have offered you Justice Holis' life in exchange for my mother's. I'd have to be mad to have trusted you—and you know it."

She was right. Eventually he'd been forced to admit it. He'd forgiven her for lying, for delaying him, for risking both their lives, as well as Justice Holis'. He just had to keep reminding himself that he'd forgiven her.

And she was taking him to the Falcon—finally. It had been Arisa who directed them off the main road, heading south on a rutted track till they stopped at a farm, a few hours before dawn, to steal a horse.

"This way, if they hear about the stolen horse, they'll look to the south," Arisa explained. She paused in extracting a bridle from the tack shed to pat the dog once more. Weasel thought she was checking on its continued health, as much as trying to reassure the beast. Only one drop of the sleeping syrup, on a bit of broken meat pie, had rendered the farm dog groggy enough to accept them as friends—or at least to keep him from barking his head off as they purloined his stablemate.

Arisa had fussed about the dosage—though why someone willing to kill four men would be so careful of a dog baffled Weasel. He might have complained, except he wasn't sure if he was speaking to her right now. Besides, he already knew what she'd say—if she'd killed those men, it would have been "for the rebellion."

Weasel had already grown tired of those words, and he had a feeling he'd be hearing them again.

As they rode through the night, Arisa refuted all he'd been told about her mother.

"She's *not* a road bandit," she told him firmly. "She's the leader of a rebellion against the tyrant Pettibone. Just like Justice Holis, except she's going to succeed instead of getting caught."

"If you think she's going to overthrow Pettibone with a few hundred bandits, you're crazier than she is!" Weasel retorted furiously.

Arisa opened her mouth to answer, then compressed her lips tightly. "Your Justice Holis didn't have the support of the country people either," she said finally. "Only some shareholders, and justices, and university men. He didn't even have the right church!"

"He had the support of the people who cared about . . . Wait a minute. What do you mean, he didn't have the right church?" The Hidden had said the same thing, Weasel remembered, but he'd been trying so hard to persuade them that he'd forgotten about it.

"You said that your Concordance of Nobles could only banish a king's adviser if they were summoned by the church leaders, right?"

"They weren't *my* concordance. And so what? The church leaders were part of the conspiracy."

"But it's the wrong church," Arisa repeated. "At the time that law was written, everyone followed the Hidden faith."

"But . . . " Was she right? "What does that matter? A church is a church. And the concordance can't happen now anyway."

"I'm just saying that Justice Holis was depending on the wrong things. None of the *people* of Deorthas were behind him."

"At least Justice Holis and his friends didn't rob innocent strangers," Weasel snapped. "Or shoot them for not handing over their purses. And the trial starts day after tomorrow!"

If Arisa hadn't assured him that she could get him to the Falcon's camp before tomorrow's sunset he'd have been frantic. As it was, he was merely . . . almost frantic. He reminded himself again that he'd forgiven her.

"Most of the deaths you've heard about were caused by other road bandits and attributed to my mother's men," Arisa told him. "That happens when you have a reputation. Mother's men hardly ever shoot anyone. They only fire if they have to, to keep someone from shooting them. They never kill just for money."

"So if someone pulls a pistol to defend himself and points it at the man who's robbing him, they're only killing him in self-defense and not for the money. I see. But even if they weren't killing anyone, you do admit they're robbing people?"

Arisa's brows rose. "You're looking for my mother because you *want* men who'll shoot people. And rebellions have to be funded, just like any government. How is robbing people on the high road, for the contents of one purse, which they probably won't miss, worse than sending the guard with swords and pistols to arrest people who can't pay their taxes?"

She waited for a long moment. "Well?"

"There has to be a difference," said Weasel. "But I'm having trouble coming up with it."

Arisa laughed. "One difference is that all the money my mother collects goes to the rebellion. No fine palace full of servants. No silk and velvet clothing. No feasts, feeding a hundred shareholders dove hearts in aspic, which cost enough to feed a hundred poor families for a week."

The Falcon's method of tax collection started to look better, but he still didn't like it. He didn't have to like it. The Falcon might be able to reach Justice Holis in time—that was the only thing that mattered.

Weasel was relieved when they crossed the main road just before sunrise without anyone having seen them. Almost as relieved as he'd been to learn that Arisa was a good rider, who controlled the big mare with ease, so all Weasel had to do was sit behind her and cling to the saddle's cantle.

Of course, a road bandit's daughter should ride well, and fight well—though he was grateful when she confirmed that her knowledge of killing silently with a knife was theoretical.

"I've never killed anyone," she admitted, in response to Weasel's nervous query. "But if I had to, for the rebellion, I'd do it."

She didn't say it with any particular emphasis, which somehow made it more convincing. Weasel shivered. He was glad he'd mostly succeeded in forgiving her.

The road bandit's daughter also knew the countryside as well as Weasel knew the city alleys. Arisa took the mare north and west for most of the day, on roads so small they seldom saw another person. On the rare occasions when they did meet someone, Arisa offered them a smile and a cheerful, "Good day t' you." Just two youngsters, riding double on a farm horse.

By the onset of dusk, they'd passed out of the area that was all fields and into a region of rolling, wooded hills. The trees were large enough to make Weasel stare—he'd thought they had big trees in the palace parks, but some of these were enormous. And the forest itself was so large that they'd ridden for over an hour without seeing fields, or any other sign of human presence. Weasel was just thinking that it would be good country for a bandit lair, when a bird's shrill whistle cut through the growing dark.

Weasel thought nothing of it—birds had been whistling and shrieking and squawking all day. But Arisa pulled the mare to a stop and whistled in return.

"What was that?" Weasel asked.

"First sentry," Arisa told him. "You think we don't post guards?"

"But don't they know you? Their leader's daughter, and all?"

"Of course they know me. It's you they don't know, and you're sitting right behind me. I could have a pistol in my ribs, or a knife at my throat, and half an army trailing behind me."

"You still could, for all they know," said Weasel uneasily.

Arisa shook her head. "If I was under duress, I'd have replied with a different whistle."

Weasel hoped she had her whistles memorized correctly. He

could feel eyes in the brushes, in the shadowed places beneath the pines, watching him.

There were three more whistled challenges, and three different replies, before they rode into a large clearing, filled with men. At first Weasel thought a clearing was all it was, but the more he looked, the more he saw.

There were tents inside the bushes, so well disguised that it took him a moment to realize they were there, and several more moments to see that they weren't real bushes. The screens of cut branches were woven around the tents so thickly, so cleverly, that a troop at a gallop could ride right through and never notice them.

The horse pen was equally well concealed, with several real bushes incorporated into its irregular shape. Even the men, and the small handful of women, were clad in browns and golds that mimicked the colors of the autumn woods. Most of Arisa's clothes, Weasel realized, reflected those same colors. In the towns and villages her coats had simply looked a bit drab. Here in the forest, she could have vanished into the undergrowth, invisible as a crouching hare.

Then a woman emerged from the largest brush pile, and Weasel's attention was riveted to her.

She wore a man's clothes, and her muscular body was held straight as a soldier's, but there was no doubt of her gender. Hair black as midnight was pulled back from a face of such angular beauty that Weasel felt his jaw sag in astonishment. Arisa's ordinary, freckled face bore no resemblance to this terrible glory.

But Arisa slid from the saddle and ran forward, and the Falcon—there was no doubt in Weasel's mind where that name had come from—opened her arms. For a moment the sharp planes of her face softened in a way that made her less beautiful, but far more human. Human enough for Weasel to turn his eyes away and think about dismounting.

A rough-looking man, who'd taken up the reins Arisa dropped, was grinning at him.

"She takes folks that way at first," he confided. "Least, she takes men that way. You'll get over it soon enough. Prob'ly as soon as you say something stupid and she tears a strip off your hide."

"That doesn't reassure me," said Weasel. "But thanks for the warning." He swung one leg over the tall mare's rump, staggering a bit when his feet hit the ground.

The man shrugged. "We owe you something for helping the little mistress get back."

He led the horse toward the pen, and Weasel approached the bandit leader.

She looked up as he drew near, and he bobbed his head in a small, instinctive bow, which was odd since he'd never had the least desire to bow to Prince Edoran. One hand still caressed her daughter's hair, but the softness in the Falcon's expression had vanished. "Introduce me to your friend, Ris."

Weasel blinked, for her accent was as thoroughly city-upper-class as Justice Holis'. He'd noticed that Arisa used her city accent when they were alone, but somehow he'd expected country speech from the Falcon. For the first time, he wondered who she'd been before, and what had brought her to such an unlikely job.

Arisa released her mother and stepped back.

"This is Weasel, Mother. He helped me escape from the palace, and we've been traveling together since. He's been looking for you."

"So I've heard," the Falcon said dryly. Weasel wondered how, but she went on. "I notice you didn't bring him here very quickly."

It was sufficiently dark under the trees that the Falcon's men were kindling fires—too dark for Weasel to be certain, but he thought Arisa blushed. "I wanted to make sure of him before I brought him in. And now I am," she added.

The Falcon looked him over. "In that case, we can probably find a job for you. You're a bit young, but we can—"

"I've got a job," said Weasel. As he spoke, he realized that it really was his job, and he wanted it back. "I'm Justice Holis' clerk."

On anyone else's face, Weasel might have taken that expression for compassion.

"Then you may not have a job much longer," the Falcon told him. "I hear Holis and his friends go to trial tomorrow. And it's going to be over pretty quick."

"I know." The relentless count of days was ticking in the back of his mind. If Arisa hadn't lied to him . . . Weasel fought down a surge of resentment. She'd had reason enough to be wary, and if he could persuade the Falcon to act, they might still be in time. "Even if they convict on the first day, they won't hang anyone till the next morning," said Weasel, trying to sound dispassionate. "The condemned are always given one night to put their affairs in order. I've got a plan . . . well, an idea, at least, for a way your men could break into the palace and seize Regent Pettibone." His heart raced.

The Falcon wasn't jumping for joy, but she didn't laugh in his face, either. "Getting Holis out in one piece is your price?"

"That's all I care about," Weasel confirmed. "What you do with Pettibone, or the prince, is up to you." Though he suddenly wondered what she would do. Pettibone probably deserved to die, but the prince . . . he might not be much loss to anyone, but he was only a year older than Weasel.

No. Rescuing Justice Holis is all that matters.

"Come into my office," said the Falcon, with quiet irony. She led them into the big brush pile that concealed her tent.

If it was an office, it bore more resemblance to that of a military commander than to the law offices with which Weasel was familiar. To one side stood a single cot, with a small chest at its foot. A sturdy-looking traveling desk, currently closed, occupied another corner, and chairs were scattered along the walls. Most of the room in the tent was taken up by a large table, with several maps spread across it. The one on top, its corners pinned with river-smoothed stones, showed a detailed stretch of coastline. Weasel couldn't tell if it was in Deorthas or some other land, for the Falcon rolled it up and put it into a chest filled with similar scrolls. Arisa lit the lamps.

The Falcon pulled up a chair and seated herself. "You might as well sit down; this may take a while. I'll tell you up front that there is nothing in the world I'd like more than to blow Regent Pettibone's head right off that scrawny neck of his," she said bluntly. "But I won't lead my men into danger unless I see a decent chance of success. Suicide is for those who have no other choice; even then it's usually a bad decision, and I'm nowhere near that point. So you may as well spill this idea of yours."

At least she was willing to listen. Weasel took a breath. "There's a secret passage leading into the old wing of the palace. We found it when . . . "

He told the story of their escape from the cells in detail, with Arisa adding things he'd forgotten—or sometimes correcting him when she thought he was telling it wrong. The Falcon asked several questions, but mostly she allowed him to babble on, more and more desperately. Weasel found no clue, in her calm face, as to what she was thinking.

"So anyway," he finished, "I thought your men could go back in through the passage and take the palace guard by surprise. Then with Pettibone in your hands"—or dead—"you could free Justice Holis and his friends. And then take over the government. Or whatever."

He wanted to continue, to describe some detailed strategy and convince her that she could succeed, but that was all the plan he had. He wiped sweaty palms on his britches.

Arisa's bright gaze was fixed on her mother's face.

The Falcon sighed. "The passage sounds like it might— *might*—be useful. But there are several things missing in this plan of yours."

Weasel's heart sank. "Like what?" She had to do this. She was Justice Holis' only hope.

"First," said the Falcon, "unless they fell for your rope-out-the-window trick, the guards who were assigned to discover how you escaped will find the passage themselves. In which case it's either well sealed, or guarded, or both. So there goes your plan."

"But they might have believed we went out the window," Weasel protested. "If they did, they wouldn't look any farther, and the passage is still open."

"All right," the Falcon conceded. "Say there's a fifty-fifty chance we can get in. Say we do get in. At that point, I've got less than two hundred men—for that's all I can muster by tomorrow—fighting the *five hundred* guardsmen Pettibone stations at the palace. And while the army may not like the regent, the palace guards are his to the last man. Granted, roughly a hundred and fifty will be sleeping at any given time. If you could somehow reach their barracks before the alarm is raised, and either lock them in or take them out, we'd be outmatched by only a little over three to two. Fighting on territory that the guards are familiar with, and we aren't. And that's assuming that the servants don't set up ambushes for us, and that there aren't a couple of dozen shareholders in the building who'd be loyal to Pettibone and willing to fight. Those odds are bad enough to start with, but when the alarm *is* sounded—and you'll note I'm saying when, not if—the army will get there in less than an hour. Maybe half that. And if they arrive before we have both Pettibone and the prince in our hands, we're all dead."

"I thought you said the army didn't like the regent," said Weasel. "Is it . . . Are they loyal to the prince?"

"That's not a question with a simple answer," the Falcon told him. "The lord commander of the army is Pettibone's man, lock, stock, and bribery. But according to . . . my sources, the general who's in charge of the troops is the one who has their loyalty, and that of most of his officers. And no one's been able to learn where his loyalty lies. I don't think he's loyal to the prince. He knows the prince. My guess is that he's loyal to Deorthas, but I don't know what that means to him. The one thing I do know is that he's not loyal to me. So if the army arrives, especially before we have hostages, we're dead."

"Um," said Weasel. The allegiance of the army was something Justice Holis had never discussed with his clerk. And at the time, Weasel hadn't cared. "Ah . . . "

That odd, cool compassion was back in the Falcon's expression. "And since the problems I've already mentioned are enough to stop me, I don't mind telling you that the final problem with your plan is that Pettibone isn't an amateur when it comes to keeping prisoners. You two can thank whatever god you fancy that he didn't really care about holding you, or you wouldn't be here. For prisoners as important as Holis and his friends, he'll post guards around their cells, with orders to kill all of them at the first sign of any escape. So even if we could fight our way through the guards, your friends would be dead long before we could seize hostages and reach the cells."

"Oh," said Weasel, chilled. "I hadn't thought of that."

"I did," said Arisa. "And I think there might be a way around it. To save Weasel's friend, we have to get him out of the cells and into Pettibone's presence before an alarm sounds, right? So we can seize all of them at the same time."

The Falcon frowned. "If you could get him there, there's a chance we could keep him alive. But I can't guarantee it."

"Well, I was thinking," said Arisa. "You know how Renn's always telling those legends about the gods, and the old earth magic and such?"

"I know that you waste too much time listening to him," said the Falcon, sounding almost like a real mother.

"Yes, but he told me about the sword and shield the old kings used to carry. He said that the shield stood for justice; that if someone stood before the king and laid his hands on the shield, he could have the king hear his case instead of the court. King's Justice, Renn called it. He said the right to demand King's Justice was still the law, after all these years."

Weasel snorted. "Even if that's true, Pettibone would probably be the prince's legal representative. And even if he wasn't, you wouldn't get much justice out of Prince Edoran."

"I know that," said Arisa patiently. "But if you demanded King's Justice for Justice Holis, they'd have to go get him, wouldn't they?"

"There's a problem with all of this," said the Falcon. "Even if the law is still on the books, and you can convince anyone to obey it, you don't have the shield. No one does."

"True," said Arisa. "But if we bring them that old shield Weasel found in the storage room . . . It looked really old. Not at all like a theater prop. If we brought that in and said it was the shield, they'd have to examine it, wouldn't they? To prove it wasn't? If they couldn't prove it wasn't, they'd have to obey the law."

"They'd ask where you got it," the Falcon told her. "And when you couldn't give them a good answer, they'd throw the shield on the rubbish heap and arrest you."

"But what if we don't tell them we found it in a pile of theater props," said Weasel slowly. "We can say we found it in a secret passage, under the oldest part of the palace. And we can show them the passage to prove it . . . "

"He'll send guardsmen straight down that passage to look for the sword, and we lose our way in—and out!" But the Falcon's voice was thoughtful. "The sword and shield were only symbols, but they meant a lot to the country people. They still do. Anyone who wants power in Deorthas would want the sword and shield in his hands."

"If you were already inside, you wouldn't need it," said Weasel. "And once the troops are in the tunnel, however many he sends, you could close off both ends and trap them there. And if you could get their uniforms . . . "

Slowly, the plan took shape.

Weasel thought he'd be too worried to sleep, but he'd been up all the last night and quite a bit of this one. When one of the Falcon's men led him to a small tent with a cot in it, Weasel lay down, preparing to run over the plan in his head . . . and fell asleep before he'd even gotten them into the tunnel.

He woke at dawn. After he washed up, and a woman tending a pot by one of the fires gave him a bowl of barley porridge, he asked her for directions to Arisa's tent.

Arisa evidently needed less sleep than he did—besides riding and fighting better—for an empty porridge bowl lay just outside the canvas door.

Her tent was smaller than the Falcon's. Four chests lay on the floor, open to show clothing, blankets, and an incongruous tangle of silk flowers. But there were still cushions on one comfortable-looking chair, and three of the tent's inner walls were covered with long swaths of cloth, dyed in bright patterns. They were so thin that those on the east glowed with the sunlight that leaked through the canvas, filling the tent with color.

The cloths that covered the west wall were already half down, and the narrow cot was stripped of its blankets, so she'd clearly been packing, but now Arisa sat at a small table, in one of the two straight chairs, and shuffled her arcana cards.

Only yesterday, the thought that she was wasting time with her cursed cards would have infuriated Weasel, but having a plan in place calmed him. In twenty-four hours they'd either be successful or dead, and either way, the die had been cast. He swallowed a mouthful of the porridge, which had been sweetened with honey. Simple fare, but not bad. "You grew up here, didn't you?"

"In this camp, yes," said Arisa. "Though not always in this place. We lived on the coast for a while, when I was younger. They were only waiting for me before moving on again, but if our plan works out . . . The rebellion, everything we've been struggling to achieve, all my life . . . It could become reality tonight."

She sounded a little ambivalent about that. Of course, this night could also end with all of them in cells awaiting hanging, which was probably why she'd turned to the cards.

Weasel finished his porridge and set the bowl aside. "Can I help you pack? You shouldn't let those cards worry you. I mean, they can be interpreted all kinds of ways, can't they?"

Arisa looked at him soberly. "You don't believe in them at all, do you?"

Weasel shrugged. "Your mother thinks this plan has a good chance, or she wouldn't try it. And she's . . . " Terrifying. " . . . she's very pragmatic."

"She's had to be," said Arisa. "But she never allows hatred to rule her. To affect her judgment."

Weasel thought that someone who would become an outlaw and raise a rebellion had to be half-mad with hatred—or at least with something. But if she was crazy, the Falcon hid it well.

"Why does she hate Pettibone so much?"

"Reasons," said Arisa shortly. "But he really is a bad ruler. He favors the city over the country, draining the farms—"

"I've heard all this," Weasel told her. "Several times. I still don't care."

Arisa sighed. "Sit down. I want to lay out your cards."

Weasel frowned. "I don't believe in them. You know it."

"If you don't believe, why not humor me?" Arisa asked.

"Because I do believe, and your actions are going to be pivotal tonight. I need to know how you're going to influence . . . Never mind."

She looked so miserable that Weasel sank reluctantly into the other chair. "Haven't you told your own fortune for tonight? And your mother's? You said it didn't matter if someone believed, as long as the person laying out the cards had some of that withe stuff."

Arisa's mouth tightened. "You're pivotal," she repeated. "Cut the deck."

Telling himself that this was nothing but the heretical superstition Father Adan called it, Weasel did as she asked.

Arisa all but snatched the cards from his hands. She drew the first, the one she'd told him represented him, and laid it down.

The hanged man, upside down as always, with blood streaming from the scarlet gash in his throat. A chill raced over Weasel's skin.

"That's the same card you drew for me before."

He had cut the deck himself. What were the odds that there was a cardsharp among her mother's men? Hmm. Not that low, actually. Raised in a bandit camp, Arisa might know even more criminal crafts than Weasel did. His nerves settled a bit.

"You look awfully pleased at the thought of me hanging," he added.

"I told you that the hanged man is voluntary sacrifice, not hanging. But the fact that I've drawn it twice means it's a powerful influence in your life. A true significator. It also means my withe is working. It doesn't always, you know."

That thought seemed to cheer her. Weasel wondered what she'd seen in the previous layouts, but she was drawing another card.

"This supports you," she said, placing it below the hanged man. "Rely on this."

The fool's tattered clothing and bright grin met Weasel's curious gaze. "Oh, great."

"Don't be silly. All the cards have deeper meanings, especially the major arcana. The fool is a wise fool—he represents the wisdom of the heart, of your instincts, rather than your intellect. So you can trust your heart tonight. It will tell you true."

Weasel's heart was telling him to run, as fast and far as he could. "Humph."

"This inspires you. How odd."

The four of stars showed a carpenter in his shop, a saw in hand, and other tools scattered about.

"Why so odd? There's a stone card below and a star card above. That ought to make perfect sense."

"It does, in a way," Arisa admitted. "But the craftsman represents the work of man's hands. Usually it indicates a physical, man-made object. Not something that would inspire you."

Which probably meant that this withe of hers wasn't as good as she thought it was. Weasel had heard similar comments from con artists playing the fortune scam, when they couldn't come up with a good line quickly. "Go on."

Arisa gave the craftsman a last, dubious look, and laid a card to the hanged man's far right. "This threatens you."

The last time Arisa told his fortune, the card in that position was the moonless night, representing Pettibone. For all his skepticism, some part of Weasel was braced to see the same card again, but the wooden hoop and spokes of fortune's wheel appeared instead.

Arisa's face brightened. "Acts of random chance, for good or ill," she pronounced. "That's not so bad. Chance plays a part in any complex plan; you just have to deal with it. And this will protect you."

She laid a card between the hanged man and the wheel—the one of waters. The fish, half in (or possibly half out of) the net, had a knowing look in his eye. Weasel had always thought he was going to make a clean getaway.

"Opportunity," said Arisa. "Though not always recognized and taken. I think this is good. I think it means that some of the random chances can be put to use, if you're quick enough to seize the opportunity."

"That assumes I'm smart enough to see the opportunity in the first place. I'm relying on a fool, remember?"

Arisa snorted, but she looked happier than she had when he came in. "This will mislead you." She laid a card to the hanged man's far left.

The skeleton-thin beggar who portrayed want appeared. Weasel shrugged. "I've been poor and hungry before. I don't think I'll be misled."

Arisa was frowning again. "There are a lot of major arcana cards here. That means powerful forces are at work. Want isn't just hunger," she went on. "Or poverty. Want is the ultimate want. In a larger context it signifies drought or famine. In a personal sense, it implies . . . well, being denied what's most important to you. A terrible need, or loss, or grief. Despair."

"We're going to get Justice Holis out alive," Weasel told her fiercely. "No matter what your stupid cards say."

"This doesn't predict the future," said Arisa. "Not exactly. It shows the influences that are acting in your life. You can use those forces to shape your future."

"You sound like every two-droplet con artist I've ever heard," Weasel snapped. The words "terrible" and "grief" were still echoing in his memory.

Arisa, scowling at the cards, paid no attention to his insult— which alarmed him more than if she'd argued. "But want, in whatever aspect, is there to *mislead* you. So you should resist it, and not let grief, or despair, or need, blind you to the opportunity. And this," she laid a final card between the beggar and the hanged man, "will guide you true."

"The book?" Weasel asked incredulously. "A book is going to save me from . . . whatever?"

"How very odd," said Arisa softly.

"I bet you're going to tell me that the book's not a book, it's the spirit of my great-granny's little toe. Her *left* little toe, that—"

"The book is knowledge, scholarship, all the good works of man's intellect," Arisa interrupted. "But that's not . . . Do you remember when I told you that most of the major arcana cards, and some of the minor ones, were really the old gods?"

"Yes," said Weasel. "So what?"

"Well, this god, the god of the book, was one of the lesser gods—the narrow god, the old ones called him, because his only interest was the affairs of men. But men cared about that, so they worshipped him. More than his power justified, perhaps. He was also the god of the city. That's why there are buildings outside the window beyond the bookstand."

The only thought Weasel had given to the book card was whether to save or discard it. But now that he looked, she was right; there were buildings in the window.

"So what?" he asked again.

"How dense are you?" Arisa demanded. "The god of the affairs of men. The god of the city. This doesn't sound familiar? As his worship became more popular, as more people came to him, the narrow god's priests changed his name. This is the card of the One God."

CHAPTER 11

THE HANGED MAN

The Hanged Man: voluntary sacrifice, for the greater good.

He'd been startled when the Falcon told a curious coach passenger that he and Arisa were both her children, and twins, though they didn't look alike.

"They wouldn't, being boy and girl, now, would they," said the middle-aged matron who'd asked. "But I can see the resemblance. They must take after their father," she added, giving Arisa a sympathetic glance.

Arisa glared at her.

The Falcon confirmed this, adding that Arisa and "Willy" were good children.

Weasel knew that his name was distinctive, and he'd used Will or William himself when he was trying to avoid attention. But *Willy*? He glowered as fiercely as Arisa, undermining the Falcon's description of "good children," but the matron didn't notice anything amiss.

When they reached the city, the Falcon let him lead the way. They found a deserted alley where she and Arisa changed back into men's clothes. Arisa looked happier in britches, but the Falcon . . . it was like pulling the cloth off a lantern to reveal the light. Yet she'd seemed more comfortable in skirts than Arisa had.

Weasel didn't have much time to think about women and skirts. He guided them over the wall and through the park to the small niche in the cliff where the great statues stood. Their white marble gleamed in the gathering dark, their faces inhumanly serene. While the Falcon greeted the men who'd already arrived, Weasel studied the statues. In those distant days the men had

11

The early dusk of autumn was falling as the coach that carried Weasel, Arisa, and the Falcon pulled into the city. Weasel had no idea where the Falcon's men might be, but the Falcon didn't seem concerned, so Weasel tried not to worry. He might as well have tried to grow wings and fly.

Granted, two seconds' thought told him that his vague notion of two hundred men thundering down the road with the Falcon in the lead was . . . unworkable, to say the least.

Once they'd packed up their camp and hidden the bundles in the surrounding woods, the Falcon had asked Weasel to give the men directions for getting over the walls of the royal park and finding the statues that guarded the tunnel entrance. But to Weasel, her command to the men to "meet me there an hour after sunset" didn't seem to be sufficient. And when it came to the most wanted road bandit in Deorthas' history traveling in a public coach . . .

It worked, though. The respectable apothecary had drawn no notice, except for the attention men paid her striking face. And somehow, clad in skirts and a modest cap, her face seemed less remarkable. Even the inexpensive locket she wore, its gold coating rubbed through in places to reveal the brass beneath, fit pefectly with her disguise. Weasel would hardly have noticed the trinket, except for the way Arisa stared at it, then looked away.

worn skirts too, though their robes were cut differently than the woman's gown. And in this trio it was a woman who held the shield, while a man held the king's sword. Yet he'd seen others with three men, and at least one with a woman holding the sword, and a man the—

"Dropped off to sleep?" Arisa asked.

"Sorry," said Weasel. "When I'm"—*panicking*—"worried about something, my thoughts tend to scurry."

"You don't have to worry about the plan," Arisa told him. "Mother may take risks, but she makes all the calculations beforehand. She knows what she's doing."

If Arisa really believed that, why did *she* look so worried? Weasel wondered again what she'd seen in the cards, but before he could ask, the Falcon came to join them.

"Almost three-quarters of the men are here, and the rest should arrive in the next half hour. A small army lingering in the king's park is going to look suspicious if a groundskeeper comes by, so let's get into this tunnel of yours."

It was the moment Weasel had been trying not to think about all day, for if the passage had been sealed, there was no plan—and no hope. He stiffened his spine and worked his way between the statues and the cliff. There were fewer leaves on the trailing vines now, but the brush was just as thick. He had to search for the door.

It was still propped open, by the same rough stone Weasel had left there. Breath whooshed out of his lungs in explosive relief.

"We just won our first gamble," he told the Falcon. "No one knows how we escaped."

She got almost two hundred men into the tunnel with remarkable silence and speed, and soon the others arrived.

Arisa led the way in—not that there was much leading involved, for the passage left no choice of direction. It still smelled of mold, and the walls had the same damp chill. Weasel didn't remember sweating so much the first time he'd gone through.

Justice Holis, he told himself firmly. *I'm going to rescue the justice, with an army at my back, just like I planned.*

He didn't stop sweating.

The first half-dozen men who climbed down the rickety pile he and Arisa had used to reach the tunnel entrance dismantled it, putting up a sturdy stack of crates for the others. Weasel and Arisa went to retrieve the shield while the Falcon's men emerged from the passage.

It was where he had left it, still wrapped in disintegrating cloth. Remembering the dizziness that had seized him last time, Weasel found himself reluctant to touch it—which was silly, for this time he was both rested and well fed. The metal was cool and rough with grit. It had no effect on him, and he breathed a sigh of relief and picked it up. It was cursed heavy.

When they rejoined the Falcon, she was standing at the locked door that led to the corridor, listening.

"I don't hear a thing," she said. "I think the boy's right; there's no one in the old wing. Even if there is, there's no help for it." She stepped aside. "Break it down."

Large, muscular men were useful. The door that had stopped Weasel and Arisa yielded to the fourth blow of their improvised battering ram—but it wasn't quiet.

As the echo of the last crash faded, they all stood, listening. Even the men who'd wielded the ram were breathing through their mouths to make less noise. The silence of centuries answered them.

The Falcon looked down the corridor, where a dozen doors opened off either side. A smile lit her harsh face. "It'll do. The next bit's yours, boy. Go on up, and remember—every man you send down here is one less we have to fight. And one less man to sink a dagger in your friend's heart, if they see we're winning."

A surge of anger stiffened Weasel's neck—as if he wouldn't have lured as many as he could into the trap without hearing that! But what she said was true, and the Falcon had already turned away.

Arisa hadn't. "Good luck," she said. "But you won't need it. This is the kind of thing you're good at. I only wish . . . "

"You can't come with me," said Weasel. "There's no reason for you to be there. It would make Pettibone suspicious, and we can't have that."

He couldn't think of anything else to say, so he picked up the shield. It *was* heavy, and awkward as well. His arms would be aching before he cleared the first corridor.

"I'll keep an eye out for the opportunity that card indicated," Weasel told her. "I'll be back soon."

He walked down the corridor toward the modern part of the

palace. The part that held light, and people, and danger, and enemies . . . and Justice Holis.

It took longer than Weasel liked to work his way through the twisting corridors, and the shield was as difficult to carry as he'd feared. He finally bent over and hoisted it onto his back like a turtle shell. It was still awkward, but his arms didn't ache quite so fiercely.

When rugs appeared on the stone floor, Weasel knew he was nearing his goal, and shortly after that he heard a man shout, "Hey, you! Where are you going?"

Weasel stopped and let the shield slide off his back. It clanged when the edge struck the floor. He rubbed his arms.

A footman stared at him, jaw sagging in astonishment. Possibly he recognized Weasel, or the shield. More likely, he was simply appalled by how dirty they were.

Time to change that. Weasel smiled.

"I have found the shield of the ancient kings," he announced grandly. "I've come to return it to the prince. And claim my reward."

The footman's eyes all but popped out of his head. Weasel waited. When the man finally spoke, his voice quavered. "Master Gerand? I think we've got a problem here."

It took longer to persuade them than Weasel had expected. When they finally gave up and escorted him to the prince and Regent Pettibone, he was accompanied by Master Gerand, two footmen, and two palace guards, one of them the captain of this watch.

The guards made Weasel nervous. But his refusal to tell anyone how he'd gotten into the palace made them nervous, so they were probably even.

Now that the waiting was over, his dread had transformed itself into an exultant, controlled terror. It was a familiar feeling, one that sharpened his eye and lightened his touch on a purse.

It also made it easier to carry the cursed heavy shield. The footmen had offered to take it, but Weasel refused to give it up. It was his price of admission.

"I shall *ask* the prince and regent if they'll see you," Master Gerand repeated for the third time. "They're dining with important men, discussing an important matter. You might have to wait, or come back at another time."

Weasel remembered what the Falcon said about the value of the sword and shield to someone who wanted to hold power in Deorthas. "I'll take my chances."

The master of household cast him a worried look, but the door to the fancy dining room was looming before them.

"Wait here." Gerand tugged down his waistcoat and lifted his chin before slipping through the door. Before it closed, Weasel smelled wine and brandy and heard the soft hum of voices in conversation. He could hear nothing through the door, but since he'd made no startling moves as they led him to the room where he wanted to go, the footmen, even the guardsmen, weren't particularly alert—and Weasel had no intention of waiting.

He gave Master Gerand several seconds to make his way to the table and whisper in the regent's ear. Then he opened the door and stepped into the room, dragging the shield with him, before any of his keepers had time to react.

"I have found the lost shield of the ancient kings." If anything, the words got more dramatic with practice. "I'm here to return it to the prince and claim my reward."

The dining room held a dozen men, clad in embroidered silk, with jewels in their lacy cravats. Every one of them was as goggle-eyed as the footman had been—including Prince Edoran.

Only Master Gerand, who'd heard it before, scowled at Weasel. And Regent Pettibone's eyes were not wide, but narrowed with suspicion . . . and recognition.

"I remember you. You're Holis' clerk."

"That's right," said Weasel grimly. He hauled the shield across the gleaming floor to the end of the table where the prince sat, and propped the dirty iron against royal knees—probably staining the pale gold silk forever. Weasel slapped both palms down on the shield and met the prince's startled gaze.

"I demand King's Justice for my master."

"You demand what?" one of the richly clad nobles asked.

"King's Justice," the prince said absently. His attention was fixed on the shield. "He wants me to judge his master."

"That's right." Weasel straightened to face Pettibone. "As is my right, by the ancient law. Which is still on the books." It had better be.

"But that's . . . Is there really a law like that?" another noble asked.

The prince took a napkin from the table, spit on it like a farmer, and began cleaning the face of the shield. The napkin came away black. Weasel considered the cost of snow-white linen and winced.

"King's Justice is the law," Pettibone admitted. "As this young clerk seems to have discovered."

Their eyes locked, Pettibone's alight with challenge. Weasel remembered that the regent himself had been a lawyer.

"However, as the prince's regent, hearing the case and rendering judgment would fall to me, not to His Highness."

Weasel didn't flinch, for he'd expected that, and curiosity grew in Pettibone's guarded expression. *What's your game?*

"But all of this," the regent continued, "including the reward, is contingent upon this shield proving to be *the* shield. An outcome I find unlikely. Where did you get—"

"It is the shield." The prince's voice was high with excitement. "It really is!"

"It is?" Astonishment stripped the cool control from Pettibone's voice.

"It is?" Weasel realized he sounded more surprised than the regent. "I mean, of course it is."

"It really is." The prince turned the shield to face the room. Across the top, where he'd been cleaning, a scene had been embossed on the iron. Weasel couldn't make out the subject, though he saw men, horses, and trees. A hunt? A battle?

"How do you know that it's the shield? Highness." Pettibone's voice was thin with excitement. Excitement, and the beginning of passionate greed. He wanted it to be the shield.

The Falcon had been right, Weasel realized. If there was a chance of passing this off as the real shield, Pettibone would help them do it—even if *he* thought it was a fake.

"You know that my father's hobby was studying the history of our family," said the prince. Weasel hadn't known it, but several men nodded. "Well, I've been reading his notes and papers."

Pettibone frowned. "I didn't know that."

The prince met his guardian's gaze defiantly. "Why shouldn't I? He was my father."

"Yes, very proper," one of the gentlemen said. "But Your Highness was saying . . . "

"Well, he was interested in the sword and shield. I think he was looking for some clue to their whereabouts. He didn't succeed, but he did find an account of some . . . marks that were put on both shield and sword to allow them to be identified. Marks known only to the royal family," Edoran added firmly, as every man in the room opened his mouth to ask what they were. "So that no one could substitute some hastily forged copy. This shield bears those marks."

"But if a forger made a careful copy he'd copy those marks, too, wouldn't he?" one gentleman asked.

"He might," the prince admitted. "It wasn't foolproof. But to make a copy that good, the forger would have to study the original carefully. And if he had the original," he nodded to Weasel, "why bother with a copy? It's not like he could claim the reward more than—"

"Where did you get this?" The cold command in Pettibone's voice made every spine in the room straighten reflexively.

Weasel bit down an equally reflexive answer. "I'll tell you that when you bring Justice Holis here, to receive the King's Justice."

"Was the sword with it?" Pettibone demanded.

Weasel shrugged. "I don't know. I didn't see it, but I didn't have time for a thorough search."

Pettibone eyed him a moment longer, then rose to his feet. "Gentlemen, as you can see, a matter of some importance has arisen. I must ask you to allow us time to deal with it."

Some of the men grumbled as they were politely herded from the room. The sword and shield! They wanted to see them, to hear the whole story. However, some of them left without a murmur of protest, and the pitying looks they cast at Weasel made him nervous.

But the prince was still present, and the guards, and the footmen, and the master of household. What could Pettibone do to him in front of so many witnesses? Witnesses who were all loyal to him? *Thumbscrews, rack, hot pincers* . . . Weasel licked dry lips and tried not to look as isolated as he felt.

When the nobles were gone, Pettibone sank back into his chair and regarded Weasel thoughtfully.

"I shall have your master brought here at once," he said. "I understand that you wish to assure yourself of his well-being." He flashed a glance at the watch captain. "See to it."

"Not only Justice Holis," said Weasel. "All the others who've been held with him on the same charges." If he left them hostage in the cells, they might be used to force Justice Holis to surrender.

"That won't be possible," said Pettibone, before the captain could ask. "Those men have been charged with conspiring against the life of their prince. There is no more serious crime, and we can't have made too many mistakes when we gathered them in."

An expert negotiator, he'd laid no emphasis on any part of that sentence, but Weasel recognized the opening offer; they *might* have made a mistake about just one justice. Still . . . how many of those men would be killed, if Weasel couldn't get them up here before the Falcon's men attacked?

But if they all came, wouldn't all their guards come with them? You could slit a man's throat in the dining room as easily as in a cell—the only difference was the price of the rug.

They could be used against the justice wherever they were. And if this didn't succeed, they'd all hang anyway.

"All right," said Weasel. "Justice Holis alone. But I see him *before* I tell you where I found the shield. And the King's Justice had better be . . . just."

"That's understood." Pettibone nodded to the guard captain, who slipped out of the room. "Though it might assist my deliberations if the sword could be found as well."

"I can't guarantee that." Weasel's heart was pounding, but he kept his voice even. "I didn't find it, though I didn't look very long. I was running out of time."

"Then I fear that I cannot guarantee the results of my deliberations," said Pettibone. He had the nerve to sound regretful, the bastard.

Anger firmed Weasel's voice. "Then I fear my memory of where I found the shield may fail me. Overcome with concern about my master's fate and all."

Pettibone hesitated a moment, then made a dismissive gesture. His hands were small, Weasel noted. Neat and well manicured. "I have no need for your master's death. And the sword and shield would be . . . useful in the current political climate. I think you can count on the King's Justice being just."

The resignation in his voice was quite convincing—if Weasel hadn't been a consummate liar himself, he might have been convinced.

The prince was convinced; he made a small, choked sound of protest. He wanted what he thought was justice to be carried out. Fortunately, the Prince wasn't in charge. A man who would bargain with justice was what Weasel needed.

Pettibone's gaze turned to him. "I didn't know you were reading your father's papers, Highness."

The prince shrugged uneasily. "Why should you? It was just . . . something to fill the time."

"Yes, but I know you have some difficulty with reading," said Pettibone. "So it seems an odd choice."

Prince Edoran had trouble *reading*? Weasel stared in astonishment, and color rose in Edoran's pale cheeks. Then his mouth tightened, and he went back to cleaning the shield.

The arrival of the guard captain broke the increasingly uncomfortable silence.

"Here he is, Regent Pettibone."

Three palace guards ushered Justice Holis into the room.

He was thin, too thin, and dirty hair straggled to his shoulders. But his ironic expression was unchanged . . . until he saw Weasel standing beside the prince.

"Ah. I wondered to whom I owed this . . . unexpected invitation." His face was still controlled, but warmth blossomed in his eyes, and Weasel felt his own eyes fill with tears. He started to run forward, but the regent's cane swung out and stopped him.

"Where did you find the shield, young man? Now."

Weasel looked at Justice Holis. The game was still on; the danger all too real.

"It was in a hidden passage, beneath the old wing of the palace. That's how we . . . I escaped. When I first found it, I didn't realize—"

"A hidden . . . There's a way into the palace that we don't know about?" the guard captain exclaimed.

"That's how I got in without being stopped," Weasel confirmed.

"Of all the . . . Excuse me, sir, but this is most disturbing. I need to secure that passage immediately!"

"So you do," said Pettibone. "And you should take a squadron of guards with you. While you attend to the breach in your security, they can look for the sword."

"I'll have to show you where it is," said Weasel. "The entrance . . .

it's tricky to find. But he'd better be here when I get back." He jerked his head to indicate the justice, but his eyes were fixed on the prince.

"He will be," Pettibone promised.

The prince's nod was almost imperceptible.

"And captain?" Pettibone added.

"Yes, sir?"

"You might remind your men that, although the reward for the shield has been claimed, the reward for the sword remains available."

The captain's face brightened. "Yes, sir!"

How big was this reward, anyway? And how many men in a squadron? The Falcon said she needed to take at least two hundred by surprise.

Weasel cast a last look at Justice Holis before following the guard captain out of the room. The justice's ironic expression had given way to a bright curiosity that was even more achingly familiar.

"Am I to take it that this is the shield?" the justice asked. "The real one? How do you—" The closing door cut off the rest of the sentence.

"Come with me," the captain said curtly.

Weasel did. "How many men are there in a squadron, anyway?"

Weasel stood outside a door in the palace guard's barracks while the captain briefed his chosen squadron—all twenty of them.

That news had shocked Weasel so profoundly that he hadn't noticed they were moving even farther away from the old wing till they'd almost reached the barracks. *Twenty.*

The Falcon had said they needed to trap a hundred in the passage and take out another hundred for their uniforms, to have any chance against the remaining guards.

Twenty men. She wouldn't do it. She wouldn't sacrifice her followers for nothing. She'd take out the captain's squadron and go back down the tunnel, and when Weasel didn't return with the sword . . .

Maybe he could find an old sword somewhere, something that would pass. . . . But Prince Edoran knew how to identify the real sword, and Weasel and Arisa had already searched the storerooms for weapons and found nothing.

Weasel leaned against the door, his eyes closing in despair. He could hear the guardsmen's voices on the other side of the door—it had taken some time for the captain to gather the men he favored for this "important duty." Now they were dividing the task, and the reward, among them—with the biggest cut for the captain, no doubt. He might be loyal to Pettibone, but he'd seized this opportunity. . . .

The image of the fish flashed through Weasel's mind. For a moment he'd have sworn that the single eye winked at him. *Opportunity.* Was there some way he could use this catastrophe? Turn it to his purpose?

Not if he stood by the door like an obedient loon and waited. The Falcon had hoped to keep the night shift out of it, but

Weasel was here, now, and so were they. It hardly seemed fair for just twenty men to split that reward, did it?

The door to the first of the big rooms, where ten men slept together, wasn't locked. Weasel looked at the snoring, blanket-covered lumps, walked over to the nearest, and shook his shoulder.

"Hey. Wake up. Those soft, withless slugs on the day shift are about to get rich."

By the time the captain emerged with his chosen twenty, the corridor was full of men, still pulling on their boots and buttoning waistcoats. Most of the night shift was present, and more were appearing every second.

The captain in charge of the night shift stalked up to him.

"My men and I are volunteering to assist you in dealing with the dangerous breach that has just been discovered in palace security," he announced. "And to assist in any other task you may need help with."

The watch captain glared at Weasel, who shrugged. "I don't want to wait a day and a half while you take twenty men on a search that needs hundreds."

"Given the urgent nature of the security breach," the night captain added, "I believe that taking only a single squadron shows a lack of judgment so severe it might call your promotion into question . . . if it came to the colonel's attention."

The watch captain transferred his glare from Weasel to his fellow officer. "My intention was to investigate the intruder's claim before . . . overreacting," he said stiffly. "If this boy is lying, it would be foolish to rouse over a hundred men from their beds."

"Well, we're up now," said the night captain, with an edged smile. "Please, allow us to assist you."

The captain of the day watch looked over the corridor, which now teemed with soldiers—most of whom were babbling about getting rich. You couldn't have stopped them with a cannon. Weasel fought down a grin.

The captain sighed. "Very well. Hogan, Marks, Lydell, bring the boy with you. And keep an eye on him. He's sneaky."

A hundred men marching through the palace corridors attracted a lot of attention from the guards already on duty. And if some friend on the night watch didn't answer their shouted queries, Weasel did. Most of them promptly decided that manning their post wasn't all that urgent, not compared to such a severe threat as a secret passage. It was their duty to help secure it, and search the place. Thoroughly. Who knew what might be lurking there?

By the time they reached the old wing, and Weasel was called to the front of the column to guide them, the passage had acquired a room full of gold and jewels to go with the sword. More than two hundred men flowed behind him, as he drew them through the tangled hallways.

Leading them down the corridor toward the storeroom, Weasel felt sweat popping out all over his body. He didn't hear a sound from the closed doors that lined the passage, but he knew the Falcon's men were there.

The door to the first storeroom had been relatched, with a

piece of wood that looked suspiciously new to Weasel's eyes. Certainly newer than the one they'd broken.

His mouth was dry. This was the tricky part. If they dragged him in with them . . . The Falcon might try to trade Weasel for one of the guardsmen, or she might not. Justice Holis was a stranger to her.

"This is where I found the shield," Weasel lied loudly. He swung the door wide, revealing a vista of dusty boxes, chests, and furniture. It was a fair approximation of a treasure room, at that.

The two officers were the first ones through, and their men streamed after them. They paid no attention to Weasel, who stood aside, politely holding the door. He knew he wouldn't have much time before the officers realized that this was only a storeroom, with another beyond it, and came back for their guide. But it didn't take much time for a hundred eager men to rush through an open door. Over half the troops that Weasel had lured into the trap were in the storeroom when the whistle sounded.

Doors flew open all along the corridor, and the Falcon's men burst out.

One of them grabbed the man in front of Weasel and threw him into the wall, then slammed his head against the stones. Another man pulled the door from Weasel's hands and banged it closed, dropping the latch. "Quick," he cried. "The bracing!"

The guardsman nearest Weasel slid limply to the floor, and he heard the Falcon shout, "No blood! No blood unless you can't avoid it. I want those uniforms clean!"

Weasel looked at the man sprawled at his feet. He wasn't bleeding. He didn't seem to be breathing. She'd said "no blood," not "no deaths."

Looking up, he saw men on the floor all down the corridor. Most of the Falcon's men held makeshift cudgels. Some of the fallen men were moaning, but many lay still. Even if they were alive now, Weasel knew that concussion could kill as easily as a sword—more easily. It just took the victim longer to die.

Some of the Falcon's men had kept their pistols and blades, now held against the heads and throats of the guardsmen still standing. Looking at their faces, Weasel suddenly understood the difference between the Falcon's method of tax collection and Pettibone's. People might not want to pay their taxes, but they did so grumbling, not in terror for their lives. And if they chose not to pay, they had time to think it over and change their minds—without dying for it.

The Falcon's men weren't decent country folk, like those who'd refused service to the guardsmen who held Arisa—they were road bandits. They were the kind of men who drank in the Empty Net.

It's all about people, Justice Holis' voice whispered in Weasel's memory. He shivered.

He couldn't trust them. He couldn't trust the Falcon, either.

"That was beautiful!" Arisa's face was alive with excitement. "I just finished the count—we've got almost a hundred uniforms! We're bound to find someone they'll fit. And there are more than a hundred guardsmen trapped in the storerooms. You did great!"

Some of the Falcon's men had stripped a door from its hinges. Now they laid it flat against the door to the storeroom—on which the soldiers inside were already pounding. They braced the door with four stout timbers, cut to fall against it at just the right angle. No battering ram would take that barrier down. Those men were trapped until the Falcon, or the army, released them.

The remaining guardsmen were pushed, or carried, into the smaller rooms off the corridor and locked in. Some of them had stirred as their uniforms were stripped off, but some of them hadn't. Some of them were going to die, and *he* had brought them here. He had set this in motion.

"If you tell me this is for the rebellion, I shall vomit," said Weasel, between clenched teeth.

"But it is." Arisa sounded startled. "Was . . . Has something happened to Justice Holis?"

"No." Weasel took a steadying breath. "Justice Holis is fine, though we still have to get him out of Pettibone's hands."

He could no longer tell Father Adan that he'd never killed anyone, but all things had a price. It just didn't seem fair that the guardsmen should pay so high for *his* master's life.

"It's Pettibone's fault," said Arisa softly. "Not yours. He's city-bred, and cares nothing for anyone else. He started this war, and soldiers die in war. These men chose to work for him, knowing what he is. Do you know why my mother's doing this? Whose portrait is in that locket she's wearing, right now, under her shirt? My father was a naval officer. That's why she's got . . . ah . . . "

"Are you going to lie to me again?" Weasel demanded. "Don't bother. I don't care—"

Arisa's chin rose proudly. "I was going to say, that's why my mother has the support of the navy. My father was killed in Pettibone's purge. He wasn't even part of that first conspiracy, my mother says. But his captain was, so he was hanged. Just because Pettibone wanted to make sure he got them all. She saw him hang. Pettibone started it."

Weasel shook his head in confusion. Was she right? Wrong? Something in between? Justice Holis might know.

But if the Falcon had the navy backing her, the odds of her rebellion succeeding were considerably better than he'd thought. He had to tell Justice Holis about this. He had to make sure Justice Holis *survived*—everything else would wait.

"I need a sword, an old sword. Something I can claim is *the* sword for long enough to get near Pettibone. Or he'll take Justice Holis hostage."

And if that happened, he didn't trust the Falcon not to shoot.

They took an old, slightly rusty sword from the hands of a suit of armor soon after they reentered the occupied part of the palace. It was much cleaner than the shield, but it might get Weasel close to Pettibone for the moment he needed to take the man off guard.

Two fights broke out, when palace guards who hadn't joined the excursion to the old wing realized that the men clad in their uniforms were strangers. The Falcon simply waved off enough men to subdue them and followed Weasel, who never even paused at the sound of clashing swords. He had to get to the justice before Pettibone realized the palace had been invaded.

He broke into a run as he neared the dining room, and the Falcon and her men jogged after him. Her hard grip closed on his shoulder when he reached the door.

"Calm down," she murmured. "No reason to run. Not if the sword's real."

She was right—they needed to keep Pettibone from suspecting anything, so she could bring more men into the room. Weasel took a deep breath. He should probably have smoothed his hair and tidied his clothes, but his hands were clenched around the hilt of the sword.

The Falcon knocked softly, opened the door, and stood back for Weasel to enter.

" . . . have it read in every village, every hamlet, even if it's only two cottages and a duck," Pettibone was saying.

Justice Holis stood near the regent, too near, but he wasn't bound. And the guardsmen were standing back, careful not to intrude on the regent's business. The two footmen and the master of household were gone, but three more guards had replaced them.

Master Darian, the clerk who'd overseen Justice Holis' arrest, stood beside his master taking notes. Too many men. Too many men who were loyal to the regent, and Justice Holis was too near him. At least the prince was seated at the far end of the table— hopefully far enough to keep him out of everyone's way.

"What is it?" Pettibone demanded—then his gaze fell on the sword. "You found it so soon?"

"We found a sword," said Weasel. "We don't know if it's *the* sword or not." He walked toward the regent, the blade held flat on his palms, his awareness fixed on the men filing quietly into the room behind the Falcon. They didn't dare come in too quickly.

Please, don't let the man wonder why Weasel carried the sword instead of a guardsman. Why it shone silver in the lamplight, when the shield, still in Edoran's hands, was black with grime.

Pettibone's gaze was locked on the sword. "Bring it here!"

Weasel came forward and laid the sword on the regent's lap, old, heavy . . . and so clearly not a match to the shield that even Weasel could see it.

He wasn't surprised when the regent's gaze, suddenly suspicious, flicked up and around the room. His eyes stopped on the Falcon's face and widened in astonishment.

She smiled. "Hello, Horace. It's been a long—"

The regent cried a warning and surged to his feet, reaching for Justice Holis with one hand while the other twisted the top of his cane. The Falcon's troops were already in motion, and Pettibone's guards as well, but Weasel knew that none of them could reach Justice Holis or the regent in time.

He hurtled all the weight of his body into the regent's stomach, knocking him to the floor, the great sword entangling both their legs. As Weasel had already ascertained, it wasn't very sharp.

Beneath the slithering silks, the regent had a wiry strength, and he twisted in Weasel's grasp like a ferret. Weasel clambered up his body, swept back a fist to punch . . . and froze as the point of a dagger pricked beneath his jaw.

His gaze rolled down to the regent's neat, beringed hand. He could see enough of the blade's grip to identify it as the top of the cane the man was always playing with.

Then Pettibone rolled to his feet, pulling Weasel against him as a living shield. The pressure of the blade at his throat never wavered.

Justice Holis was unharmed, though he was shaking his hand as if it hurt. Master Darian sat against the wall, clutching his nose. Blood leaked through his fingers. Had the justice punched him? Weasel hadn't thought the elderly scholar knew how!

But Justice Holis' freedom was the only good news; the Falcon had taken a hostage too. Prince Edoran stood in the iron circle of her arm, but instead of a knife, she pressed a pistol against his head. The shield lay on the floor near the end of the table, where the prince had dropped it.

Even as Weasel looked, the last of Pettibone's guardsmen sank to the floor, but the battle wasn't over. Sounds reminiscent of a full-scale war came from the corridor outside.

The Falcon frowned and jerked her head toward the door. Her men hurried out to join the fray, dragging the unconscious guardsmen with them.

Justice Holis looked around and adjusted his spectacles. "Let's all calm down, shall we?"

Weasel thought that was a fine idea, but the knife bit so hard he rose onto his toes to ease the pressure.

"If anyone moves, I'll kill the boy," said Pettibone. "I swear I will. And you can't kill the prince—you need him alive as much as I did."

The Falcon's smile never faded. "I only need him alive if I win," she said. "If I'm losing I'll take him with me, just to bring you down too. And you will go down without him. You're still too weak in the countryside."

"Please," Prince Edoran gasped. "Please don't kill me. I'll . . . I'll abdicate. I'll do whatever you want. Please!" His voice had risen to a wail.

A soft snort caught Weasel's attention. Arisa must have come into the room during the fighting. She stood against the wall, sensibly out of the way, gazing at the prince with an expression of utter contempt. He looked pretty contemptible, but Weasel couldn't blame him. If he thought it would work, he'd be begging too.

"The countryside," Pettibone sneered. "The countryside with its fat, superstitious ignorance, while the city works, and starves, and carries the realm into the future! The worst mistake the king ever made was to start courting those bumpkins!"

The prince froze in the Falcon's grasp. "Was that why you killed him?" he whispered.

Pettibone ignored him. So did the Falcon.

"And the worst mistake *you* ever made was to ignore the country folk," the Falcon told him. "That's why your reign teeters on a knife edge, right now. That, and killing half the navy. What makes you think I care about Holis' clerk? No one but me would dare to harm the prince. You knife that clerk, and no one gives a damn."

Weasel drew a breath to beg.

"I do," said Justice Holis. "And you . . . Mistress Benison, I believe? Despite your influence in the navy, you cannot hope to establish control of this land without the support of a large faction of important, powerful men. Not to mention the army. In short, without my support you cannot succeed. And if Weasel dies, *you won't get it*."

Weasel felt the regent's body stiffen. "*You?* You're the one . . . "

"You're the one who controls the army?" the Falcon finished for him, echoing his incredulous voice.

In some ways, Weasel realized, they were much alike.

"Let's say that certain factions in the army would be swayed by my recommendation," said Justice Holis modestly. He looked from the Falcon to Pettibone and smiled. "We intended to use the law, but we knew we couldn't count on you to do the same. We had to have some armed force at our command, if only to counter yours."

"So," said Pettibone softly. "My hostage is worth something, after all."

The prince was shaking again. He looked like he'd have collapsed without the support of the Falcon's arm.

"It won't do you much good," the Falcon told Pettibone. "The army isn't here. My men hold the palace, and I have the prince. You won't escape this time."

This time? Weasel felt as if he'd walked into the second act of a play—though no actress could have faked the burning hatred in the Falcon's eyes. Standing in front of Pettibone, Weasel caught the full force of it. She wouldn't let Pettibone escape, even if she died for it. And took the rest of them with her. In that moment, he was more afraid of the Falcon than he was of the knife.

If what Arisa said was true, if she'd watched the man she loved hang at Pettibone's command . . . She had reason.

Pettibone must have seen it too. He took three steps back, dragging Weasel with him, and something warm and wet trickled down his neck. Blood, he realized, though the regent wasn't trying to cut him. He could die very easily right now, by accident. His heartbeat thundered in his ears.

He didn't want to die.

"You may have won this round," said the regent, through gritted teeth, "but I'm not going to die today. Your Highness, get the shield and bring it to me."

The Falcon's pistol pressed against the prince's head. "No," she said.

"You can't kill him," said Justice Holis. "Whoever kills the last of the royal line would win the undying enmity of the country-side—and you can't afford that either. So let's all be reasonable, shall we?" He turned to the regent. "I'll give you the shield in exchange for Weasel. It's valuable enough to get you out of here, and easier to handle than a live hostage, who might fight or run."

"Don't!" said Arisa sharply. "That shield matters in the country-side."

"Thanks a lot!" Weasel glared at her.

"But it does matter! If he has the shield—"

"The shield is a hunk of wood and metal," said Justice Holis. "And the country folk are smart enough to recognize that."

"She's right," said the Falcon.

The hand that had grasped Weasel's elbow let go, and the knife tightened to compensate. Weasel held very still as the regent ran his fingers over the carvings on the dining room wall. A breath of musty air told Weasel that he'd found what he was searching for.

"Rot!" Weasel muttered. "How many passages does this cursed place have?"

The regent laughed soundlessly, his body shaking. He stepped back toward the opening.

The sounds of the fight outside the room were growing fainter. Pettibone heard it too—he didn't have much more time.

"I am not going to die today," said the regent. "At least, not alone. Give me the prince."

Weasel couldn't see his expression, but Arisa's face paled suddenly. "Mother?" she whispered.

The Falcon's smile was bright with malice and triumph. "I'm keeping my hostage. I care nothing for Holis' clerk."

"The shield," Justice Holis said curtly. "We'll give you the shield. Everyone in the palace knows it's been found, and anyone who challenges you will care more about damaging that than about Weasel. Anyone but . . . "

Anyone but me. Weasel guessed how the justice would have

finished that sentence, and for just a moment, an aching warmth pushed the fear from his heart.

"Cut your losses," Holis whispered. "Take the shield."

"I suppose . . ." Pettibone's grip softened a fraction. "I suppose it's the best deal I'm going to get. Enough for a start, at least."

"No!" The Falcon lifted her pistol and pointed it straight at Weasel's head. No, she was pointing it at Pettibone's head. It just looked like it was pointed at him. Weasel did not consider this an improvement.

"If he has the shield, he can start a rebellion of his own!" the Falcon continued. "It would never end."

"The shield, or the boy," said Pettibone.

Justice Holis started forward, but Arisa ran down the room and snatched up the shield before he could touch it.

"Good girl," said the Falcon. "Bring it here."

Arisa looked at her mother and her mouth tightened. She turned and walked steadily toward Pettibone, ignoring her mother's startled curse.

"Wise child," murmured Pettibone. "And you were right—I would have killed him. Give the boy the shield."

"Don't!" said the Falcon furiously.

"You said you'd let him go," Arisa protested.

"As soon as I'm free of this room," Pettibone told her. "Killing him would delay me, and there's no reason for me to do it . . . as long as I'm free."

He might even mean it. Weasel couldn't be sure.

Arisa's gaze met his, guarded, intent. Was she trying to convey some plan? If so, she failed—perhaps because the regent's knife and the Falcon's pistol were occupying most of Weasel's thoughts. She held out the shield, and Weasel fumbled his hands through the rough wooden grips.

"Lift the shield to cover us," said Pettibone sharply, as Arisa backed away. Weasel wasn't sure if the ancient shield would deflect the Falcon's bullet, but it might. He raised it, covering everything but his eyes and feet—perforce, it covered Pettibone, too.

"Stop!" The Falcon's finger tightened on the trigger. Weasel lifted the shield higher. *Would* it stop a bullet?

"Don't!" Justice Holis exclaimed. "If you sacrifice that boy to your vengeance, I swear to the One God you'll hang for it."

For herself, the Falcon might not have cared, but Weasel saw her eyes flick to Arisa. If she hanged, her daughter might follow.

Pettibone saw the Falcon's quick look too. He laughed again, aloud this time, right in Weasel's ear.

No, his mouth was above Weasel's ear. They might have been the same height, but those absurd heels lifted him almost half a head taller than Weasel. Almost.

The Falcon's finger eased back on the trigger, though the pistol still pointed at Pettibone's head.

"Let him go," said Justice Holis softly. "He's harmless without the prince."

"Don't," said Edoran suddenly. The prince's face was as white as his shirt, and the indentation of the Falcon's pistol barrel still marked his temple, but his voice was firm. "If he escapes now, he'll never be punished. He'll never pay."

He pushed at the Falcon's arm, and to Weasel's astonishment, she let him go. But the prince didn't run—he stood, staring at Pettibone.

"Don't let him escape. I . . . " Edoran's chin rose defiantly. "I command it."

This isn't the time to grow a spine! Weasel glared at the prince, but everyone else ignored him.

Pettibone vented another soundless puff of laughter, and some of the tension eased from his body. He had the shield—he would escape with his life. And the Falcon was right: With the true shield to give him legitimacy, he would start his own rebellion. He would fight, and if he won, Justice Holis and the Falcon would be killed. And Arisa, too. Even if he lost, hundreds, maybe thousands, of others would die. And Weasel was tired of this selfish, evil man.

He met the Falcon's gaze and held it.

He couldn't trust her for mercy, or honor, but he trusted her courage and her hate. He remembered Arisa saying that her mother never allowed hatred to affect her judgment.

He prayed it wouldn't affect her aim.

Weasel lowered the shield. "Fire," he told the Falcon. "Now."

The Falcon did.

CHAPTER 12

THE TWO OF STONES

The Two of Stones: the wedding. A prosperous alliance of any kind.

The thunder of the Falcon's pistol was deafening. Weasel felt the shock rip through the regent's body, and something warm splashed the side of his face. The knife sliced his skin as Pettibone was hurtled back. Weasel lifted a trembling hand to the cut. It was bleeding, but not much. Shallow. He wasn't going to die.

Three running steps took him into Justice Holis' arms. They closed around him, warm and safe, and he buried his face in the rough wool of the justice's coat. It smelled of unwashed bodies and prison food. The justice smelled as if no one had offered him a bath in two weeks, and the shield, which Weasel still gripped with one hand, was jabbing him in the ribs, but he wouldn't have moved for the world. He started to shake, but that was all right. Standing in Justice Holis' embrace and shaking was all he intended to do for the next week or so. Possibly a month.

"That was extraordinary," said the justice. "And not at all what I expected from . . . Curse you, child, you could have been killed! Why did you do it?"

For you. For everyone. For the future.

"I don't know," said Weasel. "Pretty stupid, huh?"

"Humph." The justice removed one arm from Weasel's shoulders. Weasel didn't want to open his eyes, but a pistol shot in the corridor lent him motivation.

Justice Holis stepped forward and pulled Edoran against his

other side. Weasel felt a surge of jealousy, but he could feel the prince's shaking right through the justice's body. What a pitiful thing he was. He'd been in no danger. But the way he was quaking, maybe he didn't realize that. A flash of pity dimmed the envy. Weasel had Justice Holis' love. He could spare the prince a reassuring arm.

But Holis wasn't looking at either of them.

"Put that thing away," he said quietly. "It won't do you any good."

The Falcon had drawn the second pistol from her belt, but it wasn't pointed at anyone. On the other hand, as good a shot as she was, it didn't have to be. She had hit Pettibone and missed Weasel completely.

Arisa clung to her mother, with the Falcon's left hand resting on her shoulder, staring at Pettibone's body. Her face was so white that her freckles stood out like paint. Her expression made Weasel glad he wasn't looking. She talked tough, but . . . Was this the first time Arisa had seen violent death? Weasel had seen it several times, in the lean, lonely years before the justice took him in. That was why he'd stopped talking tough.

The Falcon was watching Justice Holis. "I still have a pistol," she said. "And my men are outside."

"Ah, but unless I'm misreading the situation in the corridor . . ."

The door burst open, and a man in the dark blue coat of an army officer stalked in, followed by half a dozen soldiers. "What in the One God's name is going on here?"

" . . . I have the army," Justice Holis finished. "Hello, Diccon. This is very well timed."

Now the Falcon had a target for her pistol.

The officer ignored her. "We heard that an army of ruffians was sacking the palace. Which wasn't far wrong, come to that. We've got them pinned down for the moment, and the palace guard, as well. What we could find of them. Your doing, Holis? A bit . . . noisier than your usual style."

"No, the credit for this goes to the lady," Justice Holis told him.

"Then my hat's off to you, Mistress," said the officer, matching the gesture to the word. "I couldn't come up with a way to rescue them without getting them . . . " His gaze fell on Weasel—no, not on Weasel, on the shield in Weasel's hands. "Is that *the* shield? The servants were talking about it, but I couldn't believe . . . "

The soldiers were gawking at the shield too, paying no heed to the Falcon. "You think that's really *it?*" Weasel heard one of them whisper.

The Falcon lowered the pistol—but she didn't uncock the hammer. "Getting them out was a secondary goal for me. I just accomplished what I came for."

The officer pulled his gaze from the shield to examine Pettibone's body. "So I see. Well, since you've taken care of everything else, allow me to attend to the cleanup."

He waved a couple of men forward, and they picked up the regent's legs and dragged him out. Despite his resolve not to look, Weasel saw that the bloody hole above the regent's left eye was smaller than he'd expected. But when he noticed that the entire back of Pettibone's head appeared to be missing, his stomach heaved and he clutched the justice tighter, taking slow, deep breaths.

Killing Pettibone had probably—almost certainly!—saved countless other lives. He still wished he'd been able to think of some other way.

The prince, he noticed, watched the regent's body being taken away; his face was completely expressionless.

The officer looked at the smear of blood on the floor and grimaced. "Now what?"

Justice Holis looked at the Falcon. "She's a criminal," he said slowly. "And I just saw her shoot a man." His body was stiff with resolve.

Weasel pulled himself reluctantly from the comforting embrace. "She shot him in defense of the innocent," he said. "Well, in my defense, but I could pretend to be innocent. And we owe her. You'd have hanged, if it wasn't for her."

"You think I don't know that?" said Justice Holis. "But if we let her escape, she'll go back to banditry."

"I was thinking more along the lines of ruling all Deorthas," said the Falcon coolly. "If I signal for the rest of the palace guard to be released and tell them the army shot their regent, your Diccon might be looking at more of a fight than he can handle. Maybe enough that my men could finish off the winner. And I'm still in the same room with His Highness."

She made no motion to draw attention to her pistol. She didn't have to. And she had pushed Arisa behind her.

"No!" said Weasel. The thought of more deaths sickened him. "Please. There has to be a way." He looked from the Falcon's mocking smile to Holis' stern face—his judge's face. Surely he hadn't brought them here to kill each other, at the end of it.

Edoran muttered something.

"What?" Weasel asked.

The prince drew a breath. "Compromise." His voice was shaky, but loud enough to be heard. "You could compromise. For instance, I think that shooting was simply justice, long overdue. I could issue a royal pardon for it."

Oh, now *he was issuing pardons.* But he looked so pleased with himself that Weasel bit back the sarcastic comment.

Justice Holis shook his head. "Your Highness, people would consider any pardon you issued under these circumstances to be a matter of coercion rather than justice. It would cause more trouble than it prevented, for most of Deorthas would rise against a regent who took power by murdering her predecessor."

"Not if Pettibone's guilt could be proved," said Weasel. The country folk weren't stupid. Nor was Father Adan, nor most of his congregation. They would understand, if the truth was presented to them. "Maybe we could . . . I don't know, try him after the fact. If we had evidence of his crimes."

"I have the evidence!" exclaimed a muffled voice behind them. They spun and stared at Master Darian, who crouched in a corner, still holding his nose. Weasel had forgotten he was there. "I have papers. I have proof of lots of things he did. I can show you where they're hidden, if you let me off."

Holis shook his head. "You were complicit in most of his crimes!"

"I was only a clerk!" Master Darian wailed. "I just took notes and wrote letters. I never did anything, or ordered anything, myself. I just passed his orders on."

Prince Edoran stepped out of the shelter of Holis' arm and stared down at the man. "Can you prove that he murdered my father?"

Master Darian looked at him, clearly calculating whether or not he could get away with a lie. But the truth would come out too quickly.

"No," he admitted. "I wondered about that. I wasn't his clerk back then, but from what I've heard, I don't see how he could have done it."

"I know the man who ran the investigation into your father's death," the officer, Diccon, added. "He's an honest man, Your Highness, and he said the king's death was an accident. No doubt about it." He spoke to the prince, but his wondering gaze had strayed to the shield again. Country-bred, Weasel guessed, despite the educated accent.

The prince's face was very closed now.

"But there's a lot he is guilty of," Master Darian added urgently. "A lot. Enough to make anyone glad she shot him."

"You can't shoot a man, then find him guilty after the fact," Justice Holis snapped. "And far more important, you can't just kill those in power and take their place! If the government doesn't act within the law, then there is no law!"

The Falcon didn't care about law—her hand tightened on the pistol.

Weasel closed his eyes. Chaos and death, not only in this room, but echoing into the future. Even if the Falcon escaped, she wouldn't give up. No more than Pettibone would have. And if she died . . . He could already see Arisa, a few years older, taking over her mother's cause, her mother's place . . . her mother's contacts in the navy. Fighting the army controlled by Holis' friends . . . He had told the Falcon to kill Pettibone to prevent this! There had to be a way to bring the Falcon in with them! A way to make her something more than a bandit. To convince Holis, and the army, and the people . . .

He remembered the soldiers' eyes, wide with awe as they stared at the shield.

Weasel looked at the soldiers. They were pointing their guns at the Falcon now, but their gazes still strayed in his direction. It was only a symbol, but symbols could matter.

Weasel lifted the shield, walked briskly across the room, and shoved it at the Falcon.

"Here," he said. "It's all yours."

The Falcon's free hand reached out to grab it, her pistol tipping aside. Several people gasped. Weasel stepped away, feeling oddly light now that the burden was out of his hands.

"What in the . . . " Then she saw the expression on the soldiers' faces and gripped the shield more firmly. "I accept," she said.

"Accept what?" Holis asked furiously. "Even if it is the true shield, it was never anything but a . . . a gift the king offered his favored advisers."

"It is the true shield," Edoran confirmed.

General Diccon looked like he was thinking very fast. Weasel hoped he was a practical man.

"Perhaps it is," said Holis, "but neither you, nor your lawful regent, have bestowed it on anyone!"

"Who found the shield?" the general asked.

Arisa pointed at Weasel. "He did."

"What difference does that make?" Holis asked. "The king bestows the shield."

"The king used to," said Diccon. "But we don't have a king."

Holis and Edoran both scowled, but several of the soldiers nodded.

"The person into whose hands it was given, after being lost for centuries, has bestowed it," the general who truly led the army continued. "Be hanged if I'm going to argue with *their* choice."

He was talking about the old gods, and if he was faking the wary reverence in his voice, he was a very good actor. The back of Weasel's neck prickled. He had a feeling he'd gotten rid of that shield just in time.

Justice Holis was looking at the soldiers. They stared at the Falcon, straightening to attention. Clearly the shield mattered to them. As it would matter to all the country folk of Deorthas. Justice Holis' conspiracy had just deposed the regent the townsmen favored—without the country's support, they wouldn't stand a chance.

Justice Holis was glaring at Weasel, who realized that he had just made the first political decision of his life. He wiped sweating hands on his britches and hoped he'd never have to make another.

"She can't be regent," said Holis slowly. "Not a bandit. No matter what she's done for us. The shareholders would never consent."

"Agreed." The Falcon uncocked her pistol, resting it casually on her shoulder. "But I believe the position of lord commander of the army is about to fall vacant?"

"Yes, Mistress!" Somehow Diccon managed to make the two syllable "mistress" sound like "sir." He snapped a salute, and the rest of his men copied the gesture.

Justice Holis winced.

Weasel couldn't see Arisa, still hidden behind her mother's body, but her sigh of relief was audible clear across the room.

Weasel went over to the justice. "It will be hard," he murmured, "to get the townsfolk to accept a government that just shot the regent they liked. You're going to need all the country support you can get."

"We didn't shoot him," said Holis furiously. "We were going to act within the law. An obscure law, I grant you, but . . . Oh, rot. It seems I have no choice. Master Darian."

"Anything," Darian whispered.

"You'll give us the papers, and your testimony in court, and instead of charges you'll be banished from Deorthas. At least we can prove to the people that Pettibone should have been deposed, no matter how unorthodox our methods."

"But who will be regent?" the Falcon asked. "Whoever it is will have to agree to all these deals you're making."

"That question should be posed to His Highness," said Justice Holis, looking at the prince. "There are seven years left of your minority. Is there someone you'd trust to hold power for you during that time?"

A cynical smile touched the prince's lips. "Tell me, if I choose someone who's loyal to Regent Pettibone—which is most of the people I know—would he become regent?"

"Well . . . " Justice Holis was clearly taken aback. "Well, the person you choose would have to be suitable, of course, but—"

"So what you mean," said the prince, "is that you're going to choose a man for me."

"Someone of our faction, yes," Holis admitted. "But we'd certainly—"

"Fine," said the prince. "It hardly matters. I'm going to change my clothes now. I seem to have gotten dirty."

He stepped over his old regent's blood and strode out of the room.

Justice Holis winced.

"Well, he's right," said Weasel. "You weren't really giving him a choice."

"I know," said Holis. "But I thought if I could give him some choice, he wouldn't feel quite so helpless. I didn't expect . . . "

"You didn't expect him to see through it," said Weasel. "He hasn't had much control over his own life, has he?"

"He's a spoiled brat," Arisa muttered. "He didn't even thank us!"

It occurred to Weasel that the prince hadn't asked them to shoot his regent, so perhaps thanks weren't appropriate. On the other hand, he hadn't seemed too unhappy about it.

"He's an idiot!" the Falcon snapped. "My men are still roaming the palace. Send an escort after that young fool."

Diccon shot her a startled glance. Then he saluted again and hurried out.

Holis sighed. "It seems the dam— the deed is done. Lord Commander."

The Falcon smiled. "So it seems ... Regent Holis. Please, spare us the modest protests! You know there's no one else."

Justice Holis, who'd opened his mouth for a modest protest, winced. "It was supposed to be Sharcholder Marchington."

"Well, he's been hanged," said the Falcon. "And I'd better get out there with your friend and stop our men from slaughtering each other."

She took the shield with her when she left.

Weasel's thoughts were spinning. Was he responsible for this? Surely not—he didn't even trust the Falcon! He just hadn't wanted to see Arisa's mother die. Weasel hoped he'd made the right decision. He hoped it would be the last such decision he'd have to make, but looking at Justice Holis' increasingly thoughtful face, he feared that was unlikely.

"The One God help me," Holis muttered. "I'll have to work with that woman."

"It won't be as bad as you think," Arisa told him. "She's a good commander. And there isn't anyone else who could be regent, is there?"

"No one who wouldn't hang the lot of us for treason as his

first act," Holis admitted. "Except for some of my friends. And once they're released from their cells, they all have other duties."

"You're really going to be the regent?" Weasel asked. "We're going to live here, in the palace?"

He looked at the gold-covered dining room. He should have been overjoyed. Maybe he would be, in a year or so, when he'd managed to take it in.

"We'll have to, I suppose." Justice Holis didn't sound enthusiastic either. "If nothing else, Prince Edoran appears to need all the friends he can get. I'll expect you to help me with that. Both of you . . . Mistress Benison, is it?"

"Arisa," she told him. She looked so appalled at the thought of befriending the prince that Weasel laughed.

"Well." Justice Holis shook his head, visibly bringing his thoughts into focus. "If I'm going to take over the government instead of hanging, I'd better get started. Weasel, find a pen and some paper. I'll need you to take notes . . . hmm. And draft a letter informing all the shareholders of the change in His Highness' government. And another to the people of Deorthas, though their shareholders and town mayors will relay the news. Arisa, my dear, since the fighting seems to have ended, would you locate the servants and set them back to work? There's a great deal to do!"

His face grew brighter as he spoke, and Weasel, contemplating weeks of writer's cramp, sighed. Though after the last few weeks, writer's cramp looked pretty good.

"At least it won't be totally boring," Arisa sighed.

"What do you mean?" Weasel asked. He found pens, paper, and an inkpot in a drawer and carried them to the table.

"The sword's still missing," said Arisa. "We haven't even started looking for it yet."

"You've got to be joking," Weasel choked. "After the trouble that shield caused, you *want* to go looking for the sword?"

"Don't be silly—the shield got you *out* of trouble. But since you gave it to my mother, we could give the sword to Justice Holis here. It would make his regency more legitimate."

"And my regency will need all the legitimacy it can get." Holis sighed. "But I'd rather gain it from the support of my ruler and the populace than from a silly super—an ancient symbol. You've found a pen, my boy? Excellent. 'To the people of Deorthas. I, Prince Edoran's new regent, offer my promise . . . '"

Weasel's pen flew over the paper, and Arisa went in search of the servants. Justice Holis had a real government to build, and Weasel had real work to do to help him. The guards would probably find that cursed sword somewhere in the passage, and if they didn't, well, it had been lost for centuries. It could stay lost, for all Weasel cared. But he had a sinking feeling it wasn't going to be that easy.